ALOHA OLD FLAME

DANIELLA BRODSKY

DB CO.

ONE

EMMA

"Do we really have to go to this party? I feel like going home and putting on the TV. There's a brand-new *Outlander* I haven't even watched yet. Seen the trailer twenty times." Emma could already imagine sinking into her couch, a soft throw draped over her, the velvet pillow at her back. And of course, there was Jamie, the ridiculously good-looking male lead. How much she enjoyed watching his love scenes would remain her little secret.

A beautiful breeze ran through the palm trees, and she and Candace walked from the downtown office to some bar in Kaka'ako in heels because Candace had said they needed exercise. Halfway along their route, Emma had had enough and pulled out her trusty slippers—she loved that local Hawaiian word for flip-flops, used it even in her head.

"You are such a loser," said Candace. "And the spare slippers don't help. My grandma does that you know. And Jamie isn't real."

"I'm not a loser. It's just . . . don't you love your pajamas and comfy couch? And as for the slippers, Taylors are always prepared." Emma wasn't about to degrade her fantasy Jamie by muddying thoughts of him with Candace's reality. Of course he wasn't real; that was the whole appeal of him.

"Please don't start in with that Taylors crap again. And I knew you should have never gotten that couch. It's too nice."

"No, it's a good thing I got that couch. It's the best couch ever crafted by machine sewing care of the Swedish furniture company taking over the world, and it makes my life awesome." She smiled each time she looked at it. It was a solid thing of beauty and it was there every day for her to enjoy.

"It's all right to think an awesome life is sitting on the couch drooling over an actor in breeches if the alternative is, I don't know, cleaning bed pans, or dodging bullets in a war zone. Or even, for that matter, cleaning poo and yogurt off of the walls and saying for the twelfth time in one morning, 'Do not stick beads in your nose!' But you are a thirty-two-year-old woman who has all her limbs, is smart, and funny, and hot and doesn't have to wake up to, 'Mommy, Mommy, Mommy! Oakmeal! I need oakmeal!' Couch. *Couch. Couch.* Yup, I officially hate that word. But *sofa's* no winner either."

Emma grimaced. "Poo and yogurt? What are you doing with those kids? And thank you for all those compliments. But I have my Davenport, so I don't need a man to be happy, which is obviously what you're getting at, Mrs. Brady."

They passed by a Day-Glo stripy mural with a slick "aloha" blazing across the middle. She loved the murals; they seemed to marry the old and new cultures of the city in the best way. *Wait until you see what's just around the corner,* they seemed to suggest.

"I know that. I'm not stupid. But there's no reason you shouldn't have one. You're missing out on some seriously rewarding parts of life. Like *not* knowing the word *Davenport.*"

"And some seriously unrewarding ones, too. Do you hear yourself most days?" Emma said.

Now they both looked up to take in the mural they approached—of two anime girls in bikinis.

"Skinny bitches," Candace said. "Now what was I saying? Oh, I know. Believe me, I do know my life is not without its trials. But I can't believe you don't want to make your own family. I just don't believe it. I know you better than that. And it doesn't ring true."

"Okay, Yoda."

They passed a particularly fragrant homeless man sitting on an old beach blanket, with all of his belongings in three Target reusable totes—nice, new ones. His worn-out sign said, *Help me. I'm a veteran.*

Emma put a twenty in his cup.

Candace rolled her eyes. "You know there are better ways to help homeless vets."

"I do, but I also know not everyone fits the mold." She could remember being young and staying up all night, worrying her own dad would come home from Afghanistan that way, or not at all. Her family had been lucky, and she knew it. "And this is what this guy needs now. Back to me: I am perfectly self-contained." If she hadn't been, how would she have gotten through all those uncertain times?

"Okay, Buddha," Candace said.

"Buddha, Yoda. Do you think that name was chosen for the similarities?"

There was a deafening round of horn honking. Candace had chosen not to answer her.

"I am happy," Emma said. "I am not by myself. I have you. Besides, I just went on a date last week."

"Going to a bar and getting loaded and then sleeping with the bartender is not exactly a date."

"But it was fun." She decided not to mention that she'd slept with him only in the most literal sense. She'd passed out the second they hit her Davenport. Even more embarrassing, she could almost remember using that word to describe it. It was probably a good thing nothing had transpired, because she was pretty sure he'd stolen two twenties out of her wallet.

"Do I look unhappy? Or do you think you might be projecting your own problems onto me because you don't want to go home and clean clothes and change nappies and listen to your husband talk about how messy your house is while he sits on his butt watching *Shark Tank*?"

"I tell you too many things. And 'nappies'? Why can't you say *diapers* like everyone else?"

"What are you, the word police? You do tell me too much, most of which I do not want to hear, but that's not what I'm talking about right now. And diapers *is* a disgusting word. When we were posted to the UK, everyone said nappies, and I always pictured an adorable little baby tush."

"There is nothing adorable about diapers *or* nappies. Even if they're clean, you know that's not going to last. And you're struggling to get the thing onto the wiggly little screamer."

They turned into SALT, a place that Emma loved. As an urban development project, it was everything she admired: socially conscious—supporting Kamehameha Schools' mission of furthering the education of Hawaiian children—and design savvy, while embodying the urban, island culture of the emerging Our Kakaʻako neighborhood. It was an awesome place to spend a day, and she got some of her best ideas there at the hip coffee shop, Arvo, which a couple of *Kamaʻaina* imports like herself—these guys from Australia—had built to addict everyone to flat whites.

"Listen wherever you stand on nappies, I *am* happy. How

many times do I have to tell you? Life is not about finding *the one*. That's pathetic."

Their arrival had come at the perfect time. Emma was starting to think her subconscious mind had steered the conversation to her love life on purpose—because of those two blasted words that kept begging her to choose: confirm or delete? Oh, how her finger had hovered.

It had all started with Candace; Emma would enjoy blaming her for that when it blew up in her face.

She never would have been on Facebook in the first place if Candace hadn't scolded her for being out of touch with the people they were trying to market to. How long had Michael's friend request been festering there? And now, suddenly, it was urgent.

Jamie's call to *Outlander* seemed louder than ever, even if in front of them Bevy had an appealing beat spilling onto the street, and the smell of fried something was making Emma's mouth water. She took a step toward the entrance, but Candace stayed put.

"But what about all those things you used to say about your ex and how he was *The One*?" Candace prodded.

Emma did an excellent job at concealing her shock at the mention of Michael just as she was thinking about him. If she were a different type of person, she might start thinking conspiracy.

"Look, we broke up—how long has it been?" She knew exactly how long it had been, and Candace's eye roll evidenced how poor her acting was. "—Eleven years ago. I was twenty-one when we split. I could drink for exactly five months and two days without a hangover. And I didn't know what I was talking about. I'm sure if I ever saw him again, he would be a loser."

Emma crossed her arms.

"Like you? That would be perfect."

"Haha, so funny. Anyway, let's go have some of this fun you keep talking about." She swept her hand toward the opening, encouraging Candace to put the kaibosh on the Michael topic.

"Okay." Candace took a single step, then stopped in her tracks. "But are you seriously telling me you have *never* looked him up on Facebook?"

Now it was Emma's turn not to answer.

LATER THAT NIGHT, Emma turned off the shower even though she could have stayed in there forever. The water was just the perfect temperature, and she loved the renewing feel of her coconut scrub. She imagined old bits of her were swirling down the drain while new bits regenerated. She was a big fan of practical rituals she could rely on. The matching scent of her shampoo made her think, Yes, this is a lovely, tropical shower. It was silly, but it comforted her. It made her feel like she was home.

And she'd never admit this to a living human being, but the intensity with which she enjoyed the fragrance somehow proved to her that she'd been right to settle back here on Oahu. She'd been using the shampoo ever since she found it at that lovely store (which her father would have described as "woo woo") where that caftaned woman, Ms. Chloe, was so nice to her and always gave her those freshly baked cookies that didn't have any calories somehow, or at least that's what she said and Emma chose to believe it, because why not? Those, too, had become something she relied on. Next time she'd buy the coconut incense, too.

But it was getting late, so she left the steamy coconut cocoon. Otherwise she would press the snooze alarm too many times, oversleep and be late for work. And this did *not* make her like Candace's grandma. She had a plan was all. This was the proper way to go through life. The military way. And shut up, Candace, she *knew* her family wasn't in the military anymore. It's just good sense.

Emma grabbed for her fluffy white towel and rubbed her face into it. Her brain made the most disturbing connection: Face—*Facebook*.

No, bedtime *book.*

She used the towel to dry off her body and then wrapped it in a turban around her hair. God, could it be this hot the second she stepped out of the shower? What made those lightbulbs on her mirror generate so much heat anyway? Plutonium?

A cold glass of water, and then sleep. That was her plan.

TWO

EMMA

Her plan wasn't working. Before she looked up to check the time, she'd read fifty pages of her mystery. She had an idea *whodunit,* but she was not going to admit it to herself. This ruined the fun of the revelation at the end. She envied people who could suspend the mind's attempt to piece the puzzle together. She didn't know how that was achieved.

"It was the pissed-off agent! The bloody actor was going to ruin his entire income with his lewd behavior! But if he killed him—well! Then he'd be looking at a safe pile of residuals for life! You might as well call the book #*MeToo!*"

She tossed the paperback across the room and it landed with a satisfying plonk on the bare floor.

But the satisfaction dissipated nearly immediately.

She had a rule of never looking at her phone or computer after seven p.m. This had led to all sorts of crazy hijinks—driving to a restaurant to make a reservation for the following night, a last-minute trip to Barnes and Noble's recipe section to work out how to make a light-as-air *Paw Patrol* birthday cake for Candace's daughter.

But rules were rules.

She looked at her phone and tried to think of a way to google something without going on the phone or computer.

After twenty minutes of that, she decided it was a new world, she was meant to be connecting to it at work, and she was going to update her rules. If they could amend the Constitution, surely, she could be more flexible with her own regulations. No phone or computer after 7:00 p.m. *unless* it's for a vital purpose. If she was shocked at how quickly she bent her rule now, considering the lengths she'd gone to in the past to uphold it, she was going to choose to ignore that. Otherwise she didn't know where her questions would lead.

She'd intentionally left the new rule vague. She knew the way interpretation of the rules worked. And she ignored what this said about the changes going on in her life. Some things, most things, according to a military person, were out of one's control. She had to be ready for anything.

She padded along her Afghani runner—the same one nearly all the families they'd socialized with had, the one from the stand outside the Kabul base in 2012—and took a spot on the Davenport. It was an excellent word. She'd bring it back. Adjusting her comfy blanket and pillow, she propped the laptop atop a pillow on her thighs and got ready.

She opened the web browser and typed in: *Do normal people Facebook their exes?*

THREE

EMMA

Well, apparently they do Facebook their exes. Over a billion results showed up when she typed that into her web browser. When she took out "normal," the number was even higher.

She read through an incredible amount of those entries, until she found the one from *Psychology Today* that backed up her current desire.

IN TEST RESULTS, remaining Facebook friends with an ex-partner was inversely related to the amount of desire and longing for and negative feelings towards an ex-partner. So remaining Facebook friends meant that respondents experienced lower levels of desire and longing for an ex-partner. However, remaining Facebook friends was also associated with a lower level of personal growth. In other words, remaining Facebook friends meant that people were less likely to move on and develop new interests.

. . .

MARSHALL SPECULATES that the continued exposure to an ex-partner's comments, photos, and status updates as a result of remaining Facebook friends, may have the effect of decreasing any lingering attraction to an ex-partner. Whereas ex-partners with whom we are no longer in contact remain a mystery to us, possibly sustaining our longing.

SO, it was actually a *good thing* for her to connect with him . . . if she ignored the rest of the first paragraph. She should accept the friend request from Michael. Of course she should. But maybe sleep on it first.

And yet, her computer was already open, right there on her lap, the browser ready. If she was one of those people who left dozens of tabs open and the kind of person who often used Facebook, then Facebook would probably be open right now. While she was thinking this, her fingers did the walking. She typed "F" and the link came up and her muscles reflexively tapped the trackpad. Before she knew it, her feed was there, as if she *had* left the tab open after all.

There was a lot of reasoning going on there that she wasn't going to worry herself about just then.

Emma clicked right to the friend request list and saw his. It was now third in line to a business contact, whom she accepted, and someone named Sandy Peterson with enormous boobs and white blonde ringlets, whom she suspected was a Russian hacker trying to fish for her credit card number. She rejected that one and Michael was first in line again.

She was growing used to seeing him there. Well, not him, but his profile picture: a photo of a goat wearing a lei and surfing at Diamond Head. Which suited her just fine. She could imagine him the way he used to be.

The letters of his name manifested memories. At the

moment, they were all erotic. She could conjure up the way he used to look at her as he closed in for a kiss. Sometimes they'd keep their eyes open and look into each other the whole time. She'd come up for air who knows how long later and feel like she'd dissolved into a mass of pure feeling.

You were sixteen, she told herself. And seventeen, eighteen, nineteen. And then you never felt like that again.

Most likely, none of these memories was reliable. She went back to that psychology article so she could remember exactly how they'd worded it: "*ex-partners with whom we are no longer in contact remain a mystery to us, possibly sustaining our longing.*"

That was all that was going on here. She had to remember we were all animals who, for the most part, reacted predictably to stimuli. Still, there was something about the *possibility* of deciding to accept that gave her an incredible rush. She couldn't help smiling as she hovered the cursor over it and looked at his tiny profile picture alongside. It was as if this image and his name was a portal to their whole shared past, and she could click them forward to a shared future—if she wanted.

No, the plan was to Delete with a capital D, underlined twice. She posted that on her fridge *and* bathroom vanity in case she skipped breakfast, and when that part of the plan had been enacted, she would move on with her life. So why hadn't she done it? She crumpled up the useless paper on which she'd started to write a third reminder, planning to toss it in the recycle bin, though she knew it wouldn't be recycled because Americans did a shit job of separating paper and glass and were known for their dirty trash in places like China where this stuff was shipped off to.

Although, she thought, running her nail over the adhesive part of the Post-It, which seemed to resist her crumpling, if she accepted his friend request and scoured over his photos and his comments, then whatever brain chemical was spiking right now would normalize. But the downside, according to the *Psychology Today* article, which she instinctively understood made a whole lot of sense, was that she would be *"less likely to move on and develop new interests."* Which, given the editorial Candace had offered up earlier, would probably not do her any favors.

Michael Kavanagh.

Why did the name have such an effect on her? Even she had to admit it was a stark contrast to the warm fuzzies she got from her Davenport and coconut bath products. It was richer, deeper, more confusing, more intriguing. More *dangerous*. She needed to shut the laptop and her eyes and go to sleep. She needed to . . . A memory peeked through. Something Michael used to say in such situations. "Go to jail. Go directly to jail. Do not pass go. Do not collect two hundred dollars." She didn't know why he said it. It wasn't as if they ever got past the first few rounds of Monopoly—they couldn't keep their hands off each other long enough.

But goat pic Michael Kavanagh made a good point. She was going to lock that heart of hers behind bars and throw away the key. Maybe, she thought fleetingly, she already had.

She took a deep breath, lowered the laptop screen, and shut off the light.

Then she grabbed the laptop off her bedside table again, raised the screen, which hadn't even entered sleep mode yet, and clicked *ACCEPT*. Confoundingly, she slept like a baby.

FOUR

EMMA

"Good morning, Ms. Chloe."

Emma helped herself to a cookie while Ms. Chloe poured matcha green tea into the travel mug Emma had brought with her. Ms. Chloe's eponymously named shop was her first destination every morning. It was so kooky and eclectic, so the opposite of everything she herself was, and yet its dark, moody interior, redolent of the owner's homemade patchouli and coconut candles was a consistent draw.

"Yes, I am. I mean it *is*. I'm having a great morning. You?" Of course she was lying and doing a sloppy job of it. You weren't meant to answer that question honestly, otherwise no one would ask it. In truth, she'd slept well, but she shot right up at dawn with one question on her mind, and, of course, the first thing she did was refresh the screen to see if Michael had messaged her or posted to her wall. When Emma saw he hadn't, she watched the sun rise over the ocean in the distance. At least there was always that. And it had improved her mood, given her a dose of perspective.

But then she'd gone to the bathroom and seen the word "*Delete*," underlined twice on her vanity mirror. It had taken on a whole new connotation. And then she'd entered the kitchen and seen the same thing on her fridge. When had her apartment become so judgmental?

"Another day in Paradise," Ms. Chloe said, as she handed over the steaming mug.

The smell was a pick-me-up. She nodded. "Beautiful sunrise. And thanks for those recipes. I actually made that gluten-free cake and it was beautiful with the orange all through it." She capped the mug, a drop of tea warming her knuckle. "All right. See you tomorrow."

"Yes, you will. And maybe you'll feel a bit better."

This was the problem with staying in one place, she was beginning to think. People started to know you.

Inside the car, Emma took the first sip of her matcha latte and sighed. It was perfect. The sun was shining. Summer on Oahu, Hawaii. Permanent beach chair in her trunk. Life was great. Now, wasn't that personal growth? See, the Facebooking hadn't affected her at all. No harm, no foul. Still, that was probably enough time spent on it. Surely, she'd get some kind of alert when Michael had something to say. She shouldn't be checking obsessively. She'd have to make a decision to handle it that way, or she may never sleep past dawn again.

She pulled out of her parking space and turned on her morning radio show just in time for her favorite bit: the crank call.

"Today, we call up Jimmy's best friend and tell him he's won the lottery."

"Oh my god, that's so mean." Still she waited, gritting her teeth through the whole charade, smiling when they revealed that it was Jimmmy who told the radio hosts to "hammer him." Why did she love that bit so much? Why was it funny listening to people squirm and grow increasingly irate over their tender spots being poked at? She switched over to NPR (HPR as they called it here). She wasn't going to do any more introspection today. Couldn't she just *do* anything anymore?

But just as she had effectively closed her mind for business and was enjoying the mediocre pop song she somehow knew the words to, a thought sprung: *she* could message *him*. Something to think about. Or rather, *not* think about.

TWENTY MINUTES LATER, she rode the elevator up to the Geo Marketing offices. Five minutes after that, she was in the conference room, enjoying the last half of her matcha latte.

"All right guys. D.N.E. is coming two weeks from Friday. You know the deal: multimillion-dollar hipster clothing and accessories company. Struggling with engagement. We need creative ideas. So today I want you guys to go to your desks and come up with something completely out of the box." Her boss, Sarah White-Kalawai'a, was her usual efficient and intimidating self. Today she wore a red short-sleeved dress that looked like it was made for her. Emma couldn't decide if she admired the look or felt repulsed at the idea of so much time and money going into something like clothing.

"Isn't it *not* out of the box to say 'out of the box?'" Emma said, the comment a true reflection of the conundrum that was her boss. She'd always thought marketing was meant to be innovative, creative, but the deeper she got, the more she realized this was completely untrue in today's online world.

"Okay, haha, we've all seen how funny you are, so now can we just take this seriously?"

Candace shot Emma a death stare. She was not a fan of Emma being herself at work. "It's fine for us," Candace had said more than once, "but you're not here to make friends with people. You're here to work." She was right, of course, but at the same time, if Candace didn't work here, Emma didn't think she could face this office every day.

Ten minutes later Emma sat at her desk. A blank document loomed on the screen in front of her. *Where do I get ideas?* She looked at the local newspaper. Honolulu rail project still stalled out. Celebrity gossip. Nothing too interesting. One hour later, she picked her head up and admitted she had nothing, but she was certainly more knowledgeable about exactly how oxybenzone in sunscreens was bleaching the coral reefs.

That's something: at least she could throw her convenient but deadly spray sunscreen away and do her part to help the world, even if it meant she'd probably be too lazy to apply most of the time. But she hadn't helped her company's client in any way. The truth was newspapers were outdated, despite the fact that she saw them as neighborhood connective tissue, cultural societal connective tissue.

She wasn't even researching properly. She had to think like the target audience. She'd read the data. She knew what they were doing, and it wasn't this. It was taking place over in that other place, where that new "friendship" with Michael may or may not have begun to bear fruit. And in other places that were considered cooler than that, platforms where she didn't yet have an account.

Concentrate. Concentrate. She checked her email, read a few industry newsletters, and then cleared those search tabs and opened a new Google search. She typed in: creative marketing strategies. The first listing was Envision Global, the company for which her ex-boyfriend Michael, of the possibly burgeoning Facebook friendship fame, used to work, or perhaps still did. She hadn't thought of him in a whole hour.

But now that she had, she couldn't help but wonder what he was doing. She could easily glean his work status from his profile. She could do some digging and learn a lot about him. No. Twenty-four hours ago, accepting his friendship request had been a red line. And now here she was about to go down the rabbit hole of Michael-ness.

No clicking, no looking, no trying to remember exactly how his eyes crinkled when he gazed intensely at her. No composing direct messages in her head—were they supposed to start "Dear Michael" or did you leave that part off now? The answer was irrelevant. Because she wasn't thinking about him. She needed a new plan.

But wait. Was *Michael* looking at her profile? Trying to work out what *she* was up to? She headed to the bathroom to splash some cold water on her face. Then she got her butt in her seat to refocus on the target audience. She was a realist, after all. Michael was in marketing; he could have simply been requesting friends like crazy to increase his own audience. And here she was taking it personally. Silly Emma! Yes, that made her feel more at ease. She could almost convince herself things were back to normal.

Somehow, though, she clicked on the link for Envision Global, and typed his name right into the search bar: Michael Kavanagh. Then she deleted it and closed out that page, too. *Well done, you.*

After that, she managed to sit and brainstorm all morning, even though Michael's company—and once even his name— kept turning up in her searches. God, they must have had an excellent SEO team. Leave it to him to find the best. She'd always teased him about his perfectionist tendencies. Of course, he probably hadn't chosen the SEO experts himself, and this was the problem with this kind of one-sided reconnection; you could fill in whatever details you liked, delusional or not.

As a reward for her focused work, she allowed her finger to hover over the message button on his profile for a full minute.

She had barely ever used the feature before, but she saw how powerful it was now. With one click, she could open up a portal to the past. She was glad his profile picture wasn't of him, but that silly image of a surfing goat instead. She was not a shallow person, and understood that beauty really came from what was inside. But Michael was incredibly attractive in a way that had always affected her on a chemical level. When she looked at him, her eyes seemed to be magnetically drawn to his. She could recall her cheeks heating, thanking God she didn't blush, and being unable to come up for air for minutes at a time.

She'd read Jane Austen. She knew how frivolous and unreliable such feelings were, and she privately shamed people who didn't. She understood the biology, too. But the clinical reduction of the situation had only ever worked as long as she was away from him. Despite logic, she'd sensed what they had ran deep, was the real kind, the kind that underpinned love and brought the two together in the end, to persevere through explosive nappies and wayward teenaged daughters. She hoped in her heart of hearts that his presence was not what had actually brought her back here to live. If it was, she'd never be able to face herself in the mirror again—ignored Post-It rules or not.

FIVE

EMMA

Thankfully, the terrible thought that her having settled in Hawaii might have had anything to do with Michael scared her into concentrating on the task at hand.

D.N.E. was a slick brand. Clicking through their website was like spying on the cool kids in school. They had that Instagram star look, they understood the way the customer wanted to feel. The problem was—and this was the problem with everything—people were bombarded with messages from everyone in the world trying to sell them something. And people were starting to become numb to these messages. So how to reach them in a powerful, meaningful way?

That was her job. And it was increasingly beginning to feel like a magician's conjuring act. Often, despite Candace's jabs, what brought her to the kinds of ideas the company wrote her large bonuses for *were* the most low-tech sensory experiences—walking on the beach, losing herself in a bookshop, a museum, a vintage store. Today, after she'd opened accounts on Pinterest and Snapchat and had a good poke around, watching a few tutorials, she reached up to her bookshelf to pull down a volume her father had bought her as a housewarming gift when she'd settled back here: *The Little Guide to Leaves*. It was a tiny, square coffee-table book with painstaking illustrations. Somewhere around *White Willow* she felt a frisson of inspiration. An idea was brewing. She knew better than to force it. These things did need to be stoked, but much of the real work took place subconsciously, pulling together all the experiences and knowledge stowed in your brain. She recognized the symptoms of her best ideas by now, and she felt more than a little satisfied that one had decided to percolate now. It was just what she needed.

Before she left for the day, she pulled out an old yellow legal pad and let her brain vomit out whatever it had been brewing, withholding judgment as she did.

Hawaii
Home
Authenticity/Not Tourist Face
Community Newspaper
Our Kaka'ako
Gorgeous old Muumuus
Why does everyone love leis?
Michael

That last entry had shocked her, but only for a second. She'd been thinking of him all day, and the truth was that he had a welcoming warmth that drew everyone into a circle at his feet. It was more than charm. And she was certain whatever it was would be the missing link to this whole marketing plan. Regardless, she'd never been happier to turn off her under-shelf lights and call it a day.

. . .

THAT NIGHT she stopped for take-out Saimin, aka ramen, but with the same kama'aiana status (Hawaiian by residency) she considered herself to have—this one a mix of Filipino, Japanese and Chinese noodle traditions. While she ate it crouched over her coffee table, she once again found herself studying Michael's profile picture: was that a real goat surfing at Diamond Head? It certainly looked real. She knew how to Photoshop and this wasn't showing the telltale signs. No one else would pick something as dumb as that.

But it made sense if you knew him, which she must remind herself she did *not* any longer. Once upon a time, his nickname was goat, because of the stupid goatee he tried to grow all through senior year, only to look like a horrible experiment in hormones gone awry. She remembered a few long pube-like hairs on his chin that anyone else would have been shunned over. He was so good-looking it hadn't even dented his popularity with the girls. She wouldn't have put it past him to grow it on purpose, to see if it *was* possible to repel them.

I shouldn't click through to his page.

She thought of the *Psychology Today* article, mentally rummaging around for a good reason to support her overwhelming desire to look into his life. But while her mind was doing that, her finger had already clicked.

And she was in. The first post was of a house straight out of *Architectural Digest*; glass windows, beautiful views, ocean.

My god, what kind of a house is that for someone our age?

The accompanying post read, *Finally finished*. That was three years ago, but it came up under a cartoony image that said, *Four Years Ago Today,* festooned with balloons and bits of animated falling confetti.

Look at this beautiful life he had. Her finger and her mind had now teamed up, and neither seems to care about *shoulds*. She clicked the photo and it opened an album of quite a few images of the spectacular house. He, nor anyone else, was in any of them. It was all floor-to-ceiling windows and straight lines and solid materials. It must have been his house because he wasn't a builder, and why would he post twenty photos of someone else's house?

In a house this big, he probably had a crap-load of kids and maybe even an actual surfing, lei-wearing goat, just for posterity's sake. *My God.* Could their lives be more different?

Wait. What was she thinking? Her house was cozy and beautiful. She'd always loved that word: cozy. But now it was starting to bug her. Michael's steel and concrete were the opposite of cozy. Why was it suddenly so appealing?

She scrolled down. He was pretty private. There weren't too many public postings. There was one photo from about five months ago. He was with a woman, but Emma could only see half her face. That was kind of weird, wasn't it? Why would you put up a photo like that? She was pretty, so it wasn't like he was trying to hide her hideousness. And Michael wasn't like that anyway, hence the former pube goatee.

There must be more, she thought. In another picture she could only see a bit of the woman's profile. *Was he afraid to show her for some reason? Was she famous? Maybe his photos had been curated recently? Why would he do that?* She guessed you might go through and delete things if you were having trouble in your relationship.

She was going crazy. Looking at her watch, she saw she'd wasted twenty minutes just like that. Gone forever down the black hole of social media. No wonder this could stunt your personal growth. She was going to shut it down. Except . . .

She needed ideas for creative stuff, right?

Since she was already on Facebook, she should probably have a good look around it, see what people were after and why they were on there in the first place. This could help her think like D.N.E's target audience. She googled *Why do people like Facebook?* A great article came up from a marketing industry outlet she regularly relied on. One item that immediately grabbed her attention said, *"Loneliness decreases when Facebook users regularly update their statuses."* So strange! Why would telling people about what you're doing change the way you feel about what you're doing? Community, obviously. We are social creatures. Even introverts could reap the benefits of interaction without all the ills of doing it in person. They could feel connected and understood.

She wrote down:

Community
Aloha Spirit

That second entry happened in a flow state; she didn't even know it was about to come. But it being there was right. She could feel it deep down. She was getting there. She was going to knock D.N.E's hipster bamboo socks off. The next line she read was about a *New York Times* study on Facebook where 68% of respondents said they share to give others a better sense of who they are and what they care about. Of course! She looked back at the two entries she'd just added to her list and got a tingle down her spine. It wasn't all *"look at me"* or *"this is my reputation."* There was a human side to identity, too. And that was what interested her and she suspected it could be presented in a way that appealed to D.N.E's audience, too. Something about the way Hawaii, on its best day, could drench people in this feeling of *ohana*, or family. Being part of something greater, something that you deeply wanted to be a part of.

. . .

BY THE FOLLOWING DAY, this Michael thing had officially become a dirty secret. The emotional rollercoaster of it all was exhausting. Ms. Chloe didn't even bother trying to hide her concern over the counter.

Still, Emma erected her steeliest face to walk through the double doors and march to her desk at the back of the open floor plan. In the square set of her shoulders, there was still some of the kinship she felt with Michael. It was stupid, and all in her head, but it was there.

As she dropped her bag on her desktop, smack in the middle of the open part of the office, the placement of her desk felt like a social experiment in which she was the subject. She went through the whole morning without looking at Michael's Facebook page, though she was on the networking site checking out D.N.E's competitors. She'd noticed some new message notifications—three, in fact, in a red square flagging her globe icon. The sight immediately gave her the happy boost (due to a lighting up of her brain's pleasure center, according to the article she'd read) she was mortifyingly becoming addicted to. *I'm not going to do it. You know why? It took me years to get over him. Why would I let myself do that again? It's stupid.*

Then why did you accept the friend request?

While the presence of the friend request had been a comfort, the potential contact of the active friendship was disconcerting.

Thankfully, despite the phantom friend sensation hovering, she managed to get her concentration focused on work and surprised herself by not coming up for air until it was time to meet Candace for lunch.

"So, how's it going?"

"Good."

What Emma left out was that overnight she'd realized she could scroll through years of his feed, in fact any year of a picture he'd posted. There was even one dated 1969. She clicked on that one first because it was a 100% guarantee that she wouldn't be in it. It was of his parents on their wedding day, which brought a tear to her eye because Auntie Nita had passed a few years ago.

That had led to a long lurk through the highs and lows of Michael's last decade. He didn't put a lot up there, and she liked that about him. It was one of the things she'd always liked about him. He played things close to the vest. He was a beautiful little mystery, waiting to be discovered. It wasn't that he was vacuous or anything like that. It was just that he didn't need to tell everyone everything. She was surprised at the reaction she was having, angered almost. After all this time!

This was stupid. And dangerous. And yet, she felt connected to him, all these miles and years away. The commonalities between them made her stand up taller. He would think social media was dumb, too. Hence the goat photo, the lack of interaction, and the dearth of posts.

She wanted more than anything was for none of this to show on her face.

"Any dates on the horizon?" Candace asked.

"Aren't you interested in anything besides my romantic life?"

"What romantic life?"

"Seriously, that's enough."

"Seriously, that's enough," Candace mimicked.

"What are we five?" Emma said.

"That's why you love me. I make you feel so young."

"No, it's because you spend all your time with kids that laugh every time you say poopy nappy."

"It is pretty funny."

"There is this one thing," Emma said.

"Oh yeah? What?"

"Never mind. It's stupid."

"Come on, Poopy Nappy, you can tell me."

"Fine. But you have to promise not to tell anyone."

"Who am I gonna tell? Poopy? Or Nappy?" Candace said.

"Good point. Okay, well, remember how we were looking for all those creative ideas that nobody managed to come up with yet?"

"Yeah."

"Well, I found myself just kind of wasting time doing all this stupid stuff on Facebook." Where was she going with this? Despite Emma's every instinct telling her to keep this mortifying business to herself, here she was spilling it.

"Yeah, you and every other person in our department."

"Okay, good. And I kind of sort of connected with Michael." And there it was. Maybe it was time to admit she was struggling with this sudden Michael resurfacing.

"Oooooohhh, intrigue!" Candace smacked her hands together.

"No, no no. It just got me thinking. We had that . . . that . . . thing, didn't we? It made me feel, I don't know."

"Yes, yes, you do know. And I bet it's the reason you love your comfy blanket so much. And that god-awful night shirt you think is sexy."

"Never mind." Candace always knew how to hit the tender spot. She should have kept it to herself.

"Come on, come on," Candace said.

"I shouldn't go back there." She couldn't look Candace in the eye.

Thankfully, the waiter brought her fish tacos and Candace's pizza, so she had something to focus her gaze on.

"Well, you were in a really bad place after that."

"But I don't know. I haven't met anybody I cared about since," Emma said. She smoothed her napkin over her lap and hefted a taco to her lips. She tasted the perfect combination of crunch, spice, rich aioli, and tangy lime.

"Or maybe you have but you just don't let yourself."

"That's stupid. How could I not let myself?" Emma didn't go in for all this overcomplication people seemed to spend so much time on.

"By finding something wrong with everyone else? Imagining they pale in comparison to the fantastic Mr. Michael."

Emma rolled her eyes. "The heart wants what the heart wants, doesn't it? That's what you always say."

"Sure, sure. But that's for me. And normal people."

"Listen Poopy Nappy, I went around for almost a decade moping about that guy, and you were working overtime to get me to just let loose and forget about him. 'Don't worry if they aren't Michael!' you said. And now I have done all that, and you're saying, maybe you weren't doing it right. Maybe give it another shot with Michael!" She noticed she was shouting. Perhaps there *might* be something slightly more complex going on.

"Look, I'm not saying anything. All I'm saying—yes, I know—you're not being all you can be."

"Now who's thinking outside the box?"

"You know what I mean."

Emma did know what she meant.

"By the way," Candace said as she turned to go. "Who contacted whom?"

"Why does that matter?"

Candace turned back with her eyes bugging and her head at an angle that wasn't doing her any favors. Apparently, that look was meant to speak for itself because she didn't say another word.

Emma flicked her back the bird. As if it had physically hit her, Candace coughed, her shoulders jerking.

Emma's inability to stop considering pursuing the Michael connection was enough to scare her off Facebook for the rest of the afternoon, during which she'd made some excellent progress in the *ohana* idea for D.N.E. But later that night, when she'd pulled her knees up on the couch to enjoy some *Outlander* binging with Jamie, she could not ignore the fact that the fringes of her cozy blanket were now irritating her; not only that, but they smelled gross. Like . . . like vomit. Why would her blanket smell like vomit? She tried not to scratch at her arm and then swallowed down the bile percolating before balling the blanket up and shoving it in the washing machine with an excess of detergent.

And later, when she slipped a decadent chocolate square onto her tongue for her evening treat, it wasn't as satisfying. It melted quickly and then went bitter as she swallowed the last of it. And when she cozied up into bed, she found a tear, big enough to stick her thumb through, in her favorite off-the-shoulder nightgown. She'd have to get a new one. Maybe her apartment really was revolting against her.

When she looked on the internet for a replacement, the nightshirt had been discontinued. That, finally, brought a tear to her eye. She blinked it back, of course, but she could feel that things were changing, whether she liked it or not.

SIX

EMMA

It was Friday before Emma knew it. The week had been challenging. She'd tried to tell herself that she wasn't using all her effort to avoid her Facebook notifications, which now numbered 11, just in case one was from Michael. It was good not to move too quickly on this whole Michael thing. She wasn't stupid enough to think he was living in that giant house alone, after all. So why rush herself to heartbreak?

But Candace didn't let her get away with it.

She texted, though she sat less than fifty feet away.

What's the good word from Mr. Michael?

Don't know. Haven't had a chance to check my Facebook notifications in a couple of days.

Bwahaha! That's funny. What are you afraid of?

There Candace was, poking again at her tender spot. Well, she wasn't going to bite.

At work, she started trying to master the art of posts that didn't look like posts, meaning "organic," real things that people like to say. This was apparently the current trend in social media marketing. That is to say, try hard to act like you're not trying hard. It did strike her that all this posting was required to get a genuine feeling across, but she chalked that up to too many voices screaming into the void; with the amplification the internet posed, such posturing was required to be heard. She ignored the voice in her head that kept asking, *"What's the point?"* Bills, food, survival—those were the point.

She posted asking if she should try bubble tea. She'd seen the Mr. Tea place with the mustache logo when she and Candace had gone to the party the other night in Kaka'ako, and was intrigued by the milky drinks in plastic cups that looked like they had marbles at the bottom.

Been debating some major life questions and need help: Should I give bubble tea a go?

She linked the location of Mr. Tea to the comment to get a feel for product/consumer interaction. Right away, she saw the notification pop up at the corner of her screen. Candace had commented.

Yes. It's bubble tea that's the answer to all your problems.

First Emma replied, Fuck off, but then she realized this wasn't a private message and deleted that.

I know, right? It's the small things.

Of course, Candace did not reply. But two high school friends did.

Eewwwww! Don't do it. Super gross, brah. Like globs of slug sliming their way down your throat!

The second one struck a different note.

Hey, I live right near there. Next time you're there give me a call.

Then a third: *You look great!*

The simple post had taken off. But what was even more surprising was that she really did enjoy the banter. It hadn't felt pointless or like posturing at all, though she was up against a pretty strong mindset instructing her it should. Maybe she *was* afraid . . . of change. Fucking Candace.

That afternoon, she had a bit of prep time scheduled with Fucking Candace, who'd been charged with prioritizing the pitch strategy for Monday's meeting. Emma had been dreading it all day.

But when the Michael topic came up all Candace said was, "Be open to the possibilities."

"That sounds like some kind of yoga garbage."

"I know. I got it from a yoga class. But I think if you genuinely pay attention to the words and concentrate on what they mean, you'll see that you haven't been open at all. You've found a place that fits comfortably, that fits in with all the rules, and you love it. But it just might be possible that you can love something else as well, maybe even more. You can choose to be your own person without having to make your life the opposite of what it was growing up."

"I don't know about that," Emma said. "Besides, I didn't think you were into Dr. Phil anymore." But it did actually make sense, though she wasn't about to tell Candace that.

Instead Emma showed her the post about the bubble tea and explained her motivation—the organic touch, the *ohana* push she was percolating for D.N.E.

"Sure, it's a great idea, but everyone is trying to get their community going. How can we make this one stand out, is the question?"

Emma tried to expand on the *ohana* take and realized she needed more concrete examples—images, music, a representation of the best of that lifestyle message in practice. She went back to her seat to track it down.

Forty-five minutes into her mission, while arranging a couple of printouts on the workspace opposite her computer monitor, she heard the Facebook Messenger pop-ding. She'd told Candace, the only one who used this chat feature with her, that she'd check in with her fifteen minutes from then. Why would she be rushing her?

When she turned back, the notification badge had faded, so she opened a Facebook window on her browser and clicked on the lightning bolt. Down popped the list of recent messages, all from Candace, except this new one. It was a message from Michael. There was the goat image, just in case she had any confusion. The caption said, *Ignoring me?*

The immediacy of the sudden interaction, without having any time to prepare, threw her for a loop, and before she knew it, she'd typed an answer and pressed return.

Aloha! What do you mean? Have you tried to contact me?

Oh god, that was incredibly stupid, but she only realized it the second she couldn't take back the words. She'd accepted his friend request. He would have been notified of that. And probably one of those 11—now 14—messages awaiting her were from him.

Nice to see you haven't changed.

She wanted to pretend those words had no effect on her, but that was impossible. He knew her. Not only that, but he'd loved her once. And she'd loved him. In that moment she was sure that love couldn't have vaporized, the way she'd told herself so many times. She caught her reflection in the window beyond and saw a huge, stupid grin on her face. Immediately, she forced it away and straightened up. The thing to do was to steer the attention away from her.

And I can see from your profile pic that you look pretty much the same.

Hahaha.

The grin was back. What a wonderful thing to so effortlessly make someone laugh, to cross distances and feel, well, intimate.

So, back to my original question. Why are you ignoring the three posts I wrote on your fb page?

Three?

I'll get you up to speed: I'm here, in Kailua. And I'd love to see you tonight.

Here????

Won't your mansion co-habitant be jealous? No. no. She deleted that.

Have to check my calendar.

No new Outlander tonight.

Fucking Candace. But it meant he'd been looking at her page. Just as she'd been looking at his.

Hahaha.

So?

Okay.

There was never any other choice. The interaction had been pure instinct, the way she wished most interactions in her life could be—no need for preparation, awkwardness, or falsity. Instead, it was delicious, more-ish even, and had the undeniable haze of fate around it.

If she was already this enthused, she was well and truly screwed.

SEVEN

EMMA

Emma didn't want to make a big deal about what she was wearing. She just pulled on a pair of jeans. Sure, they were the jeans that fit her best, made her butt look high and tight. And she slipped on a tank top—yes, it was one she'd spent a little too much money on, cut in such a way as to elegantly show cleavage without looking slutty. As for makeup she wore just enough to cover the dark spots and brighten her complexion, and highlight her green eyes and what she was often told were her best feature: her full lips. She even ran a curling iron through the ends of her hair before brushing it out into softer waves so it didn't look like she'd tried too hard. Because she hadn't.

She was ready way too early. So, she poured herself a wine to calm the nerves and tried to think about the second meeting with Candace that afternoon. She had been trying very hard not to feel giddy or antsy, but her heart had been thumping so intensely she'd looked down a couple of times to see if it was visibly pulsing. She was certain she could see it.

Candace had been impressed by the mood board Emma

created on her Pinterest account, which she projected onto the wall of the darkened conference room.

When she was through, Emma felt sure the campaign was a winner. The pictures spoke for themselves. It was a community anyone would want to be in. She turned the lights on and prepared for some praise.

"But how does this translate to D.N.E?" Candace asked.

Though she'd known this back to front earlier, she couldn't articulate her thoughts properly. "Live events with a relaxed, friendly, inviting vibe. Spotlight the products that bring the core of the brand into right now."

"Sounds like a lot of jargon."

Emma tried to go back to the photos while she pointed at the screen.

Intimacy is the word she had been struggling to pin down. A group of people who *got* each other, who reached out and made that clear, even through something as small as appreciating the same style. It was that mutual appreciation—no matter the content—that created the community feeling. But *ohana*, she felt, took it to another level. Maybe it wasn't possible to achieve online. Maybe that had been her error.

In the end, Candace had red-lighted her, and explained they were going another way. Candace went through the highlights of the campaign pitch and told her she'd email it to her to prepare for Monday's meeting, where they were going to nail down the to-do list for the successful D.N.E. pitch.

Once she was back at her desk, she picked up her phone to check if the email had come in, but the loading indicator went around and around and her mind began to travel.

Michael's Facebook friend request was probably the most disruptive thing that had happened to her life since her relationship with Michael ended. Immediately, her thoughts began to pull in the *what if?* direction. For a minute she just let them go there. She was supposed to be open, wasn't she?

Her memory settled on the night they'd said their goodbyes before she left for Paris. Not too far from where she now worked, she had been at a party at the home of a friend—Amy, the one who'd told her to look her up if she was at Mr. Tea. There had been beer and beautiful live ukulele music, and the kind of pink and orange sunset Hawaii was famous for. Emma had worn a hibiscus in her hair and about a dozen leis around her neck. She remembered thinking, *I can't go, can I?* And it was kind of like Michael had read her mind.

He'd said, "It's not going to be easy going somewhere all by yourself. But think about it. You can't go where your parents are going to be, because it's not where your school is. And you made this choice all by yourself, because that's what you wanted to do. That's what you talked about more than anything. You're going to go to Paris, a place that's always stuck out in your mind, that you've always loved, and you're going to do so well in your classes there, and you're gonna grow from it, and come back and tell me all about it."

So why had making her own choice for the first time actually feel like the opposite of freedom? It was as if the freedom itself had trapped her. She'd never trusted anyone in her life the way she'd trusted him. He'd always, always known her.

They weren't deep words he'd spoken, but they were accurate. And the unspoken part was true, too—she might be making a mistake, and they were young, and it might mean the end of them. That was just common sense. Her parents had sat her down plenty of times to make sure the thought had solidified in her brain. It had. But she treated it as the most unlikely outcome. In fact, every time she told herself it was a possibility, she felt her body physically reject the idea, all the while convincing her parents and herself that she understood.

What she hadn't counted on was that Michael had accepted it so completely. So, she'd been well and truly shocked during his visit five months later when he'd dropped her from his life forever. He was right about one thing: she had grown, but it wasn't as if she'd changed 100 percent after she incorporated new aspects into her life; maybe initially, when she was swept up in all the novelty, she'd felt unrecognizable, but then she'd worked it into her core, and that was when the real growth had happened. She'd kept some of herself and had felt pride in that. She recalled how much straighter that had made her stand. She'd been sure Michael would feel it, too.

And that pride would always bring itself back here, to Hawaii. She was sure of that. Her father had been stationed here for three years of her high school education and what could she say? She took to it. While her mother complained about a lack of parking, the unhealthy food, and the fact that no companies would ship products to the island state, Emma herself appreciated everything. For instance, there was nothing else like a *shaka*. Nothing in the world even compared.

The more French she'd become, the more Hawaiian she'd stayed. She'd worn tight T-shirts and shorts with slippers, and she'd stuck out among the sleek Parisian girls, but in a good way, she thought. Her hair and makeup were better now—no one on-island could do a better messy chignon in one minute flat—and she had better T-shirts and shorts to choose from, but the point was, she'd evolved in her own way. In a lot of respects, she couldn't have found two more opposing cultures. But this helped her to look at the nuances of both of them, and in the end, led to a greater appreciation of home.

At the close of her first year abroad, she'd had to decide if she was going to go home for the summer or take the dream marketing job she'd been offered at the expensive, elegant shoe brand she'd been interning with. She still had her shoes from them and used to say she wouldn't trade them for anything. But she never really meant it. The heels were too high and they pinched her toes, so she barely wore them. It wasn't as if she hadn't bought her tickets, as if she wasn't ready to go home. She'd known that's what she wanted to do. She's never been so sure about anything.

Emma's doorbell rang. She'd at least wanted to sort out what she thought of it all from this perspective before he arrived, and leaving it unfiled gave her a strange, untethered feeling. Regardless, Michael was here.

The swing of the door brought his scent her way. He hadn't changed his body wash—that hypermasculine stuff that came in a black bottle and had names like, *Solid* or *Steel*. The scent held memories that sent her chest swirling. She had to remind herself she had no idea why he was looking her up now. There was clearly someone else, and maybe he just needed a friend, or someone who reminded him who he used to be. Likely, it had nothing to do with her. Only, this was Michael, and he would have considered her feelings on the interaction. He was always intuitive that way.

"Hi!" Her voice came out squeaky and high-pitched.

"You look beautiful."

She could say the same to him. The unshaven looking shave, the pointed eyebrows, the watery brown eyes, the longish hair pulled back. This had been a bad idea. She'd forgotten how *manly* he was, and how that had always made her want to launch herself into his arms.

"See you started drinking without me." He leaned in and kissed her just far enough along her cheek that it was almost her neck. The move could have been innocuous if he didn't know that was the spot that drove her nuts. His free hand embraced the small of her back and she pretended it had no effect on her.

"TGIF." She backed away and held up her glass. Could she sound any lamer? "Would you like one?"

"I got your favorite beers: Longboard." He held up not a six pack, but a case, by two fingers.

"Why, Michael, I'm a lady now. I don't drink *beer*." Who was she channeling? Scarlett O'Hara? That would fit perfectly with the into-his-arms launching and the hair curling.

"Right." He showed himself in and rested the case on her kitchen island, which overlooked the living area. He pried open the box and popped off two caps using just the edge of her countertop and handed her one. This bottle de-capping was an old trick of his and she wouldn't give him the satisfaction of being impressed, especially since these days her counters were granite.

"This isn't a frat house, you know."

He didn't respond with so much as a shrug. Instead, he made his way to the Davenport, while she stole a peek at the well-filled-out back of his jeans, and her favorite bit of him, his shoulder blade beneath a white T-shirt. This was even more difficult than she could have predicted.

She placed the beer bottle down on the counter and took her wine to sit next to him. She'd finish the sauvignon blanc first. That would show him. Sure, it would.

He smirked at her drink, but once she sat next to him—not too close—he clinked her glass with his Longboard and took a long sip. She turned away as he licked his lips.

"To old friends," he said.

"To old friends." So there you had it. That's all this was. Lick-lipping old friends who curled their hair. Enough time had gone by and he was hoping they could do the platonic thing. He probably missed her as much as she did him, and he was hoping they were both at a point where this could work. Could it?

In seconds, he was up touring the room, inspecting all her

keepsakes. There were photos from lots of places. She'd lived all over as a military brat. Thailand, Australia, New York, Arlington, Kansas, Alaska. Some places she could barely remember. But her time with Michael, though he was conspicuously absent from all the memorabilia in a physical sense—she'd hidden the photos he starred in long ago—had been part of almost every Hawaiian memory that she had displayed there.

"Oh, I remember this!" he said, pointing to an aerial beach shot. "You were so gung-ho."

"I know."

"You always wanted to jump out of a plane. 'I'm going to jump out of a plane! I'm going to!' Like you came out of the womb wanting to jump out of a plane—"

"Did I say I know?" She came up behind him, but not too close.

"—Or at least you wanted everyone to think you did."

She flashed him a scowl.

"You never did like it when I had you pegged," he said.

She cleared her throat. What exactly was going on here?

He picked up the photo and waved it around, and when he turned and met her eye, Emma had the sensation the symbolism of little her shaking in his alpha-male hand was too close to reality.

"So, what happened?" he continued. "We got up there, and you sucker-fished yourself onto the side of the plane and refused to let go."

"How many times does a person have to relive this?"

"Come on. Don't take this away from me. I never get to tell this story anymore."

"Go on. You seem to be enjoying it so much." She tilted her head and bulged her eyes, like she couldn't wait to hear what would come next.

He frowned quickly, then caught himself, smiling hugely. "I

said, 'I'll tandem with you,' but they said, 'We're only 150 feet; a five-year-old girl just jumped out there.'"

"That's not what they said!" She was surprised to hear her own laugh.

Now his smile sat more naturally. Encouraged he continued. "Anyway, it's Hawaii so, *ahui ho* and there we go, I pulled you, they shoved you, and you screamed bloody murder. I said, 'Open your eyes.' And you looked down and there was Diamond Head, the sand, the hotels, all the places we knew like the backs of our hands. You grabbed for my hand and you squeezed it." His hand twitched. Was he stopping himself from demonstrating said hand squeeze? How did he remember it all so clearly? Exactly as she had? Why did she feel disappointment at the missed moment for the hand squeeze? She shook out her hair and tucked a strand behind her ear.

He made his way back to the Davenport—no, it was just a stupid sofa, wasn't it? Already out of style—and over the back of it, now grabbed her hand, to demonstrate. What was he playing at with such a premeditated delay? She felt her cheeks warm and raised her glass to camouflage.

"You saved me, you were the hero. Hero Michael." She fluttered her lashes, so he would see how sarcastic she was. Even while she was trying to save face, there was Scarlett's accent again.

"Yup, that's me." He backed away and let her go.

"What have you been doing?" she asked, feeling for more solid ground. She sat on the *couch*, but not too close.

"Working. You know me, working in finance, making the big bucks, day in, day out. Don't really have many aspirations beyond that. Just really wanted to make money."

"That's not true. You make money for your family—that's the point." She hadn't known she was going to say it—the unsayable. Considering how quickly the temperature in the room had risen, it was probably for the best.

Michael didn't speak.

"You don't have to talk about that if you don't want to."

"I don't."

"Okay." But there it was between them like a valley of swords. He had a family, and she wasn't part of it.

He went back to the mantle, so she couldn't see his face. They stood in silence. Maybe this had been a mistake.

"You want some chips?" she asked his back, his ridiculously sexy shoulder blade beneath his shirt.

"Nah."

"Okay. Music?"

He turned around. "Sure. What have you got?"

Emma carried the laptop to the coffee table and they sat together before it on the sofa. She opened her iTunes library and scrolled through. "Oh, I got one for you!"

She started with something safe: "Remedy" by Jason Mraz, the song they had been lulled into loving that summer so many years ago, from its continuous radio play on the two pop stations on Oahu. It was conspicuously unromantic, and she chose not to dwell on what her selection might say. It was a great opener.

They started to sing at the same time and looked at each other, continuing on. She felt her own head bobbing in time with Michael's. This went on for several minutes, until they breathlessly made it to the song's bridge, and she turned to sink back into the couch only to be surprised by his hand on her wrist, pulling her into a dance. He was always a good dancer, he had the natural, slow hip rhythm, the internal sway.

He used to say, "You'd better not tell anyone about that," because none of the other guys knew how to dance and they'd make fun of him. The moment the music began, he'd pull

Emma into his arms and that pull they had was steel, absolute steel.

It began arms only and she thought, *okay, I can handle this.* The lyrics started up again and he surprised her by pulling her closer. Now she was too aware of the feel of his tee shirt on her bare arm.

Thinking fast, Emma tipped the last of her wine into her mouth and tried not to run toward the kitchen, where she had the pretense of grabbing her beer to save her from the reaction that had clearly spread to the apples of her cheeks. Woah. That had burst out of control almost instantly.

If she wasn't careful, before she knew it, she would be in his arms again, just like all those nights. As she swallowed her first sip of icy lager, she looked up at him and there it was, that same connection between them. What had she been thinking, agreeing to this?

The song finished and, hot-faced, she made her way back to the couch and the laptop to choose another song. But he beat her to it, opting for The White Stripes' "I Don't Know What To Do With Myself."

The riff had a trancelike quality that evoked long hot nights on Kailua Beach, sand between her toes, Michael's chest at her back. She jumped at the guitar riff.

He pulled her toward him again.

Just say it: "Don't you have a wife?" And for the love of God, pull away.

He stroked her hair from her eye. If he leaned in to kiss her, she didn't think she'd be able to fight it. The anticipation had been what, eleven years in the making? And the disembodied online contact had only intensified whatever Michael fire she'd kept burning all these years.

The White Stripes moved on to "In the Cold, Cold Night." This one had an even more sultry quality and the air around them seemed to heat up. She didn't know what to do with it. Her body was shaking everywhere. She didn't even kid herself that he wouldn't notice.

And then he looked at her in the way he used to; what exactly had changed in his expression she couldn't pin down, but it was too much. Finally, she had enough terror at her reaction to this and her mind's spiral down the rabbit hole of what it all might mean that she pulled away.

"Hey, why don't we go and take a walk?" Emma heard herself say.

She hadn't truly considered this before, but what if he had children? She didn't want to be a home-wrecker. It didn't say much on his Facebook page, but she wouldn't post about kids if she had them either, not with all the weirdos out there, so that was no guarantee. Too dangerous. All she needed to do was come out and ask, and yet, she couldn't. For a can-do girl, she was certainly failing miserably tonight.

"You want to take a walk?" His breath was audible and this, too, caused her to move farther away from him. It was too intimate, his breath.

"Yeah. It'll be fun." The slight upward tug at his brow said something altogether different.

IN MINUTES they were across the street and making their way up the cliff path.

"Looks pretty different here these days, doesn't it?" he said.

"Well, you know how the locals are; they hate it."

"Aren't you a local?"

"Yes, but I've also lived in other places, and to tell you the truth, I think there're some benefits to having a modern clean center to the area." Emma enjoyed the fresh fruit and seafood at the Whole Foods market and the funky cafés that had cropped up.

"What about all the people who get priced out of the areas where they grew up?" As he said this, Michael's palm swept over the multi-million-dollar houses across the road.

"I'm not saying that isn't an issue. But you also can't have a lawless place where you know drugged out guys are just screaming at people in a parking lot."

"What, you mean Darryl?"

"Yeah, Darryl. People coming here paying five hundred a night for a room don't know who Darryl is. They just see some crazy guy coming at them, calling them a cunt."

"Didn't know he liked that word. That's the way it is. *Aloha.*" He reached out for her to step over a large crack in the path. She pretended not to notice and grabbed the hand rail instead.

"No, that's not *aloha*. That's just not taking care of our society."

"Things are changing anyhow, for sure. A lot of tourists in this area, too. That's kind of new."

"I don't see it as such a bad thing. It keeps the economy growing, opens up new jobs, I mean, obviously this neighborhood is doing great or they wouldn't be opening a brand-new shopping center."

"People don't like change around here."

"Well, they're not the only ones." Why had she said that?

"Speaking of change, how come you decided to settle back here?" he asked her.

"Oh boy, that's a long story." Why had she said that? It wasn't a long story at all. In fact, it had been instinct. She'd turned down the job in Paris that summer after she'd finished out her last term in Paris, and yes, she'd hooked up with some guys after her split from Michael, enjoying the novelty of the French words whispered in her ear, but her heart hadn't been in it. She began to see a future alone as date after date disappointed her. No one compared to Michael. And she began to fear she'd be washed up at 21. She'd never been a settler, and so even if she'd wanted to, she just didn't have it in her to be with anyone who made her feel less than she did with Michael. And that was no short order. She never voiced the theory, because she realized it sounded naive and dramatic, but in her mind, Emma had made preparations for a solo life. And that solo life was never going to be based anywhere but Kailua.

"We've got time, walking up this beautiful road, toward Lanikai. Just me, you, and maybe some turtles."

As if she was going to share it now. And with him!

"Well—" How was she going to tell this story while leaving out his role in it? She had to, though, didn't she? He wasn't a take-no-for-an-answer kind of person, and besides, she needed to give him a reason, or he'd likely work out the truth for himself.

Since she'd been thinking about it earlier, she began with the decision not to take the job at the shoe company. The second she'd announced it to her boss, she'd realized how pathetic she seemed, running back to America. She'd been planning to take it, but on the way to the office that morning, she realized she was only doing it to prove she was someone that she really wasn't. She wanted to go home, only she didn't want anyone—including Michael and herself—to think she was doing it for him. She wasn't supposed to base her decisions on a man. And it would have just looked desperate if she'd gone home. He'd have lost respect for her. And yet, she'd humiliated herself and done it.

She left all that out and said only that "It was a hard decision." But when she backed up to the part about what happened during his visit to Paris that summer, she told the truth. She didn't even know why, but as she did, she sensed the distance between them closing. Weak as it made her look, it was the right decision to come clean. Even if this was just a start at friendship, wasn't honesty the best way forward? She ignored the simplicity of the thought and plodded on.

"—And there we were, out on the Champs-Elysees, with all the tourists, at this street-front bistro, having our beautiful wine and beautiful meal."

"God, 'beautiful, beautiful, beautiful.' You really like that word, don't you?" he said.

"That's what it was, and then you dropped a bomb on me."

He stopped walking, shifted his legs into a wide stance. "I didn't drop a bomb on you."

"You did. You said, 'I think we should have our freedom while you're here,'" Emma said.

His hand balled up at his thigh. "Yes, that's what I said. But don't tell me you didn't think it, too."

"No. I didn't."

Michael's chin sank. He was serious.

"There weren't any French gay-looking dudes that you wanted to hook up with? Please. I saw your friends and how they looked at you. " And there went the hands-on-hips. Emma had taken psychology: she knew men did this to make themselves look bigger, fluff up their non-existent feathers. Good. If she was upset, he should be too.

She picked some imaginary lint off her shirt so he wouldn't see how angry this replay version was making her. "That's ridiculous. They all knew about you and how I felt about you." She tried to keep her voice level.

"Makes you more appealing. I don't think you know how they talked about you when you weren't around." If possible, his arms shifted out wider. So, it still hurt Michael, did it?

"Does it matter how they talked about me?" Emma leaned

on the hand rail and grasped her own hips. She wasn't going to be on the defensive here.

"Yeah, it does. When I'm thousands of miles away holding you back from all the things you wanna do. I don't want to be that guy when I'm only 22 years old. I don't want to be that guy now." For a second his chin lifted, his face tilted, eyes sincere. And then it was gone.

"You were never that guy."

"Of course I was. I saw the way you looked at me when I didn't know what Châteauneuf-du-Pape was. You were embarrassed of me." If she wasn't mistaken, his arms were reaching to cross, but he stopped them, leaned on the arm rail himself, stretching his grip as wide as possible. She had hit him where it hurt, hadn't she?

"Where is this all coming from?" she asked. Judging from his perfect pronunciation of the wine, he'd clearly thought about it plenty. How had she missed that?

"Oh, please. You had to walk me through things that I could tell you were so embarrassed that I didn't know."

"That's ridiculous." But even as she said it, she realized it was true. She had been caught up in all the novelty and the Frenchness and the sophistication. Though she'd been the newbie plenty of times by then, there was something about Parisians that was different. She loved it—the genesis of the *je ne sais quoi*. She wanted to consume it, grab onto some of it for herself, take the deficient parts of her and French them up, even while she wore her T-shirts and shorts like a badge of honor. It was hard to explain.

She'd been busy proving something to herself, even if she wasn't sure exactly what. But she hadn't treated Michael that way. Had she? She'd definitely treated herself that way. She remembered ironing out her G's and the exaggerated syllables she'd picked up in the Midwest postings, and she'd tried to speak more often of her time in Germany and Japan. When she'd mentioned Hawaii, she'd had an annoying habit of using the local words no one would understand, the words that had made her feel like an outsider when she'd arrived on island.

The metropolitan French seemed so self-assured, like they knew Paris was the world and why would they ever want to live anywhere else, and that made her more insecure than she'd ever been in her life. They never even asked her what the Hawaiian words meant.

"It's in your head," she insisted. "I've been the newbie plenty of times and it's a weird feeling, alienating. That's probably what was happening." Now she caught herself tilting her head. She wanted to be right, but also, she saw he'd been hurt, and it must have been bad if it was still raw.

"Was it? From the second I got off that plane you were so cool with me, like you didn't like me anymore, much less love me." His volume had lowered suddenly for a couple walking by hand-in-hand. He nearly swallowed the last words.

Emma winced, shaking out her hair to cover the reaction. "How could you say that?" Was he right? She'd been so concerned about her own identity, could she have overlooked his feelings completely? "Maybe I took you for granted a little bit, but if I did it was only because you were like my own arm, such a part of me." That was a bit too revealing for her tastes.

"Maybe that's the problem. I'm not a part of you. I'm myself," he said, and started walking again, leaving her to follow.

"Why didn't you say any of this?" Couldn't they have talked this out all those years ago?

They walked silently in single file for a few moments, then reached the highest point of the walk, where it curved around the old lighthouse. The cars whipped past and tourists pulled *shakas* for selfies with hibiscus clips in their hair, or wrestled the incline on rented bikes. The sun was truly set by then and she glimpsed the first visible stars.

She stopped walking, leaned once more against the railing.

"Please. You can't make somebody love you," Michael called over his shoulder. Then turned to face her. Was he looking for her reaction?

She wasn't going to show him one. She made her face neutral when she delivered her response. "I guess you're right. You can't. Good thing you left and threw away all those years. Congratulations. Because you knew best. I definitely didn't love you." Let him take that however he wanted to.

"You loved me, but not enough for where you were headed. It was the right thing to do."

That was it. Screw his opinion. She couldn't contain herself any longer. "Right thing? Didn't love you enough? Are you fucking serious? Do you know how long it took me to get over you?" She was well and truly angry now. The wound had been picked and it was oozing all kinds of shit now. Shit she hadn't intended to deal with—ever. She should have clicked *DELETE*. Then the wound could have festered quietly on its own until she died a slow, unforeseen death instead of being blown apart by this sudden bombshell.

"You don't think it was hard for me?" he said, crossing his arms.

"I'm sure it was. You and Corner Girl."

"Corner girl?"

Shit. Why had she said that? "Yeah, your lovely Missus."

"What do you know about that?" His pointed eyebrows always gave away his anger, and from their sharper angle and strain now, she could see she'd gotten to him, too. "I see things haven't changed all that much. Gone and lived around the world and come back and you're the same old stubborn Emma you've always been. Only you have fancier hair now."

"I don't have fancy hair." She chose to go back to ignoring the Missus. There was enough to juggle without that.

"You do. And I like it better the old way."

"Maybe it's time you went home."

"Maybe it is."

EIGHT

EMMA

The walk back to her apartment alone was long and there were too many happy Friday night revelers around for it to be therapeutic. She noticed he'd continued down the other side of the hill, though he would have no business there. She turned around a few times, but he hadn't looked back, and then she was so far down the hump she couldn't have seen if he did.

Still, she was calmer—if just as thrown—by the time she sat down on her sofa to pore over photos of her hair over the years. Surely it hadn't changed that much. She knew she shouldn't have curled it. This, at least, was something she could sink her thoughts into without too much pain. The rest of it, she couldn't touch yet.

By the time she went to sleep, she realized her hair had just become more finely layered, a better adaptation of her assets and shortcomings that served to put her best face forward. It was the normal kind of tweaking that came with age. Only, Michael hadn't been around for the gradual transformation. She began to think, *What if he had?*

For a few moments, she allowed her thoughts to follow the path they'd begun to tread during her argument with Michael. She hadn't liked herself very much during her time in Paris, and it was probably why she'd come home in the end. She was broken down after her stint there, as if the person she thought she'd been all her life, the Strong Taylor Progeny, was all a façade held up by the scaffolding of her mother and father, and once her parents were out of the picture, it had all came tumbling down.

But surely she wouldn't have treated *him* that way. That's ridiculous. No matter what was going on inside, she had always been master of the game face. *Walk the walk,* she'd tell herself, though never in front of anyone else. To find she hadn't been able to pull it off—at least to Michael—made her feel stupidly vulnerable.

But she'd felt so close to him precisely because he could see into the real her. There was a slow-clapping respect in his insight which overwhelmed her if she thought about it too much. Why couldn't she just accept that his spotting of her weakness had been a side effect?

Because he'd rejected her. That's why. *Please kokua can you meet me at my apartment?* How many times had she said that in Paris, though she'd never once said it on Oahu? She winced at her words even now. They were the words of someone trying to be something, even, or maybe especially, if they didn't know what that something was.

After that painful indulgence in her worst fears, Emma spent the rest of the night distracting her brain from such thoughts with television. She just wasn't ready to go there. And there was no good reason she should.

She had a hangover on Saturday and binged on a new Netflix series that wasn't actually that good but offered the necessary distraction. On Sunday, after an early evening bath, she looked over the presentation Candace had emailed her and picked out something to wear for the following morning. She even cleaned her kitchen and bathroom and ran a vacuum over the floors. She was done feeling sad. She was moving forward, being proactive. Making things happen.

ON MONDAY MORNING she skipped Ms. Chloe altogether —too afraid of another insightful reading—and made her own tea instead. She'd left the teabag in the travel mug and it had grown bitter. Before the meeting, she went to the kitchen to get a fresh cup, but the old one splashed all over her white blouse, and she wound up being late, entering the full conference room with a stained, wet, clearly rubbed-at splotch, and she'd forgotten altogether about the new tea, which was sitting in the kitchen growing cold.

"Everybody, except Emma. I'm glad you could make it to the pre-meeting meeting on time." Sarah was miffed. The negativity washed over her in a dense wave, and she began to perspire despite the arctic climate control. She realized this was a day-two hangover.

"I'm so sorry, I'm so sorry."

"Well, let's close by congratulating Stephanie for pitching the winning idea for Friday's meeting with D.N.E. You'll pick your team, Candace will assign the tasks, and we'll take it from there. Emma, you come to my office after." *Stephanie?* Stephanie of I'll parrot your ideas back to you so reassuringly you won't even realize I didn't bring anything to the table fame? Blasphemy. Still, Emma was late. And clearly distracted. At the moment, she wouldn't choose herself to lead a team either.

To Candace, Emma leaned in to say, "I'm in big trouble, aren't I?"

"Well, you've never been late before, so that should work in your favor. But what happened to you? What's going on?"

"I just overslept." Candace looked dubious, and with her extra tight top-knot, which she swore scraped ten years from her appearance, her entire hairline lowered a couple of inches with her sharp squint.

The room emptied out.

"Just overslept, huh? Miss Military precision, 'if you're late you die,' simply didn't wake up on time? Okay, but that's like me saying, 'I forgot to put my clothes on before I came to work. Does this have anything to do with Michael?"

Emma jerked back like she'd been slapped. She'd practiced the move earlier, in case Candace said something like this. Her BFF could be annoyingly perceptive. "*No-uh*. Why would it have anything to do with Michael?"

"Okay." Candace's *okay* was worse than her questioning.

"Nice bun!" Emma said to her friend's back, only to get the finger—not even a backward glance to go with it.

WHAT FOLLOWED WAS a long day at the office. Her idea was better than this duo of bullet points she'd been assigned.

- *Recruit a celebrity to serve as brand ambassador*
- *Post a contest for interdisciplinary artists, who will then be* promoted on the site

She understood the motivation behind these two tactics. They were in keeping with industry standard practice these days—seduce people into wanting to be as amazing as the brand ambassador, or at least feel associated with him, and use inscrutable cultural images to make people think there was something so cool going on with the brand that they couldn't even understand it if they tried.

They were both bullshit tactics that fed into the cultural problems of this world she lived in. She was giving air to Billy Joel's fire doing these things. She didn't light it, though, she reminded herself, trying to cheer up. No, she couldn't even crack a smile. Everything—this slimy marketing, the circumstances and reactions that had led to the end of her relationship with Michael, which were now being exhumed—seemed to be connected, part of the same, larger problem. Again, though, she couldn't articulate exactly how. And she had a terrible feeling this inability to name the problems might be a root cause.

For now, she should be focused on things she *could* do. She wanted to create something inviting, rather than seductive. *Aloha.*

She looked at the mood board Candace had created for the PowerPoint. Image-wise, they'd gone with long-haired surfer guys in hoodies, or in various stages of undress, looking like they couldn't give a shit, and girls with beach waves and featherweight T-shirts or bikinis with the requisite no breasts. Did people still feel seduced by this? Probably. The brand ambassador would simply take that to a whole other unattainable level that would make everyone think their lives sucked in comparison.

Her interoffice messaging system binged. It was Hilary, Sarah's assistant.

Sarah will see you at 1 instead.

Emma let out a long breath. Good. This gave her some time to get into a better headspace.

The way to do that was to concentrate on the task at hand. Now, where was she? Oh yes. To her credit, she'd tried with Candace, but now that she saw this by-the-book marketing plan, she understood she hadn't stood a chance by trying to make waves. This wasn't a wave-making time in the world. Unless you had a gun, of course. What a depressing world. She had one of those rare moments when she wanted to throw her hands up and walk away from it all. What was the point?

No. No. She didn't want to get sucked into the *"I'm just one tiny person; I'll never make a difference"* hole, so she stopped herself right there. Sure, this was just marketing. But it set an enormous cultural tone. She *could* make a difference. And she *would*.

She had to begin with the tools at her disposal. There were these two bullet points. She could pick the *right* ambassador. And she could pick the kind of art that spoke to people, instead of scoring points on its obscurity. That was a start.

By the time she left for her lunch at a funky fish joint, her spirits had begun to lift. She sat and enjoyed her poke bowl, looking around at the people who shared her city and didn't seem the least bit afraid of parasites in raw fish, even at supermarkets that regularly sold past-due meats. Inside her subconscious mind, the creative process was doing its thing, and she was on the right track. She could feel it.

And then she heard her Facebook messenger pop-ding.

She would ignore it. Because there was a chance it was Michael. And she couldn't deal with whatever it was he was stirring up right now.

To her credit, she walked back to the office with her phone tucked inside her purse and on silent mode, though the poke was churning in her stomach.

NINE

EMMA

"Sit," Sarah said, extending a hand to her guest chair, strategically placed, no doubt, according to the guidelines of *How to Win at Work and Intimidate People*.

Emma did as directed. "I apologize again for being late." This, to a woman whose hair reflected the light in silky straightness, while everyone around her was poofed out like a pack of frizz monsters.

Sarah flicked her eyes up to meet Emma's then looked back down at the print-out on her desk. "That is not a good look. But uncharacteristic of you."

This was a fair assessment. *Finally.*

"And it brings me nicely to why I wanted to see you today." *Right.*

Emma tried not to gulp, but if she didn't swallow, she was going to choke and that would be worse. She chose to reach down and scratch at a nonexistent itch on her ankle while she forced down whatever was retracing its path up her esophagus.

"What you bring to this team is divergence. Just like your

talent assessment promised when we hired you. And divergent people add an integral mix to the team—"

A smile was creeping to Emma's lips. Was this a good thing she was meeting about? She certainly never thought anything good could come out of that tedious talent assessment.

"Until—"

Here it comes.

But it didn't come. She seemed to be working up to the *until*. But what could that mean?

"People are raised to believe problems have a single, correct solution. This is not the case in the real world. But that's why you get all these copycat campaigns, packaging, slogans. And they work. Until they don't. People get overloaded with them and they don't penetrate anymore.

"Creativity gives our lives meaning—and most of the interesting, important, and human elements of life are the result of creativity. 'When we're creative, we feel we are living more fully than during the rest of life,' I read in a book once. *'The excitement of the artist at the easel or the scientist in the lab comes close to the ideal fulfillment we all hope to get from life, and so rarely do.'*"

She hit a little close to home with her impressively memorized words. Emma felt along her cheekbone and turned to the window. She was positive Sarah knew her words made Emma think about the direction of the D.N.E. campaign.

"But the benefit for the rest of us," Sarah continued, "is that we get to enjoy the fruits of this divergent, creative thinker, so we can apply it in the way that the creative is often allergic to."

This made sense. And seemed as close to a dream job description as one could get. *Go. Be creative. We'll do everything else.* Yeah right.

"Which brings me back to that *until* I was leading up to . . ."

Again with the *until*. If it was anyone else dragging this out, she'd be barking "Get on with it already!"

Instead, Emma composed herself and turned her gaze back to her boss. This was where it was going to get serious. And undreamy.

"Until the divergent creative feels stifled. And then they begin to doubt the meaning of the work they are doing, the life they are living even."

What the fuck? Was she being followed by a private investigator? And did this have anything to do with her apartment going haywire on her?

"It's textbook."

Oh, well that makes it all much better, doesn't it?

"So, what's she going to do about it? This is no doubt what you're thinking."

Yes. Throw in a couple of F-bombs and it was precisely what she was thinking. Emma inclined her chin and tried to keep her body neutral, though she was beginning to want nothing more than to crawl into a ball and disappear. There was no point in waving any of this off. Clearly this was reckoning time for Emma Taylor. That was one thing the events of this week had made certain she understood.

"I need you to take things to the next level. You need to make the most of your assignments for this D.N.E. pitch, and if you show me you can do that, especially in a campaign that isn't to your tastes—"

"I—"

Sarah showed Emma her palm. "Don't. I know how you feel. And you're right in a lot of ways. Anyway, knock my socks off there and you will have a different, tangential role in this company—incubating the creative ideas in your own space. But you have to realize you don't work in a bubble here. We are at this company to grow our clients' businesses. And that requires a lot of moving parts, and a lot of data and painstaking application. So, you have to show me you have what it takes to be not only a creative, but a marketable creative. It feels like a dichotomy, I know. But you must bridge the gap. It is often difficult, nearly impossible to put your finger on the exact intersection of marketable creativity. And that's where working collaboratively kicks in. We're a team here. And you're an important part of it—just like Candace is. We all have our part to play. So, let's see how you do. And get you to that next level."

Sarah had clearly finished her pitch, evidenced by her boss's swift chair swivel to the filing cabinet behind her. "Now go. There are still socks in need of knocking off."

Emma left the office honored and pressured, excited and also disturbed by how well she'd been read. And perhaps mostly because she hadn't been imagining it: her life was coming to some kind of precipice. And the marinating phase felt like it was over. It was time for action.

The messenger alert hadn't been from Michael after all. It was an offer for $2 off her first bubble tea at Mr. Tea in Kaka'ako. Someone was doing their marketing right. Though it *was* creepy how much they knew about her. This was just another reason why she'd avoided Facebook for so long.

AT FIVE O'CLOCK, going over the perfect candidate list she'd compiled for the celebrity spokesperson and the exact right call for art that would blow everyone's mind (no pressure; well, yes, pressure, but this was good pressure—exactly the sort she thrived under), Emma hopped into her car and raced back home. She told herself to chill out. She'd worked hard all day and now it was time to step back from the task and get some perspective. Historically, this would mean she'd wake up knowing the right choice.

So, she turned on the computer and looked right at Michael's Facebook page. How to explain it? Even after the argument, perhaps especially in light of it, the look of his stupid goat profile picture, and even the strung together letters of his name, felt like a wave of comfort softly crashing over her, refreshing and well, *right*. There was no telling herself it hadn't felt good. It clearly did.

Why had they been so angry? What she'd said was true, but probably, his argument had some merit, too. She'd been crushed when he broke up with her, and that had overshadowed all the details leading up to the split. It had been a time of growth, if she looked back on it now, with the characteristic push and pull, swell and crack that came along with it. She'd not acted in a way that, in the long run, did her any favors. But she *had* grown. So, who was to say it was wrong?

In the meanwhile, there was this non-combative Facebook page of Michael's, where she could pore over his sparse words, so few that it was as if they were *inviting* her to read between the lines to see what he really meant, what he was really all about. He wasn't here on this social media page. He was the Michael she spent the night with over the weekend, he was the Michael she'd lost herself to in kisses and embraces, and even simple grazes of a thumb, the Michael she'd exquisitely lost her virginity to—with much less pain and much more pleasure than she'd heard of anyone else experiencing for their first time.

He hadn't been a virgin, of course. Just look at him. And he was very sexual. He told her he'd been fifteen (!) when he lost it. The girl had been older—seventeen, a senior—and Emma knew who she was. She saw her sometimes at a smoothie joint she may have co-owned or perhaps just managed. She was stunning and wore flattering fitness clothing all the time and it seemed, from their perfect fit, like the clothing had been custom made for her, or maybe she'd been the muse for the designer who'd conceived it. And sometimes, childishly, Emma sat at a small corner table, sipped her smoothie and sent thoughts out to the girl along the lines of: *He loved me. Not you.* It never made her feel better about anything. In fact, when she left, she was usually ashamed and saw how pathetic the behavior was, swearing—falsely—that she'd never do it again.

Why do you even care about that anymore?

The most recent such occurrence had only been a month ago.

Most likely, what Emma was doing now, decoding his Facebook page, was similarly ridiculous. Still, it was hitting the spot. And she couldn't help but think the posts on his page had been created, or omitted, with her in mind. *What do I want Emma to think of me? To know about me? To wonder about me?* Like he was speaking in code to *her*. She was the only one who really got it. She knew that was crazy. But she also felt it might be true. His friends' comments were so off the mark, she could convince herself he was lost without her. No, Jimmy from Boston, whose profile picture showed a shaggy-haired blond in a Bruins jersey, Michael wasn't likely to be telling you whether he paid more than "two mil" for the *Architectural Digest* house.

TEN

EMMA

The next day she was groggy and, despite wanting to skip Ms. Chloe's intuitive assessment about Emma's detente with Michael (still, neither had messaged the other), she required a matcha latte to get moving. Ms. Chloe merely nodded sagely. That could be taken any way a person wished, Emma assured herself. Still, she grabbed her drink and raced out as quickly as possible. She'd spent the best part of the evening dissecting Michael's Facebook page in lieu of reaching out about the sticky offline reality of the other night.

She was pissed off that he'd made his own decision about what she needed, and they'd wasted all these years apart because of it. But when she fixed her attention on the few photos of him online, she realized he might have also felt regret. Had he sacrificed his own happiness for what he'd mistakenly thought would be hers? She didn't know how to put that into words, especially since some of the things he'd said about her behavior had given her pause.

How to work out such a thing? First, she'd tried to think

whether she recognized any of the clothes he was wearing, or if everything was new. She couldn't say precisely why she'd begun there, but it seemed like familiarity would be a good base. In two photos at Boston Harbor, he was wearing a well-worn Hawaiian Island Creations T-shirt, one that she had bought him for Christmas junior year. Did he think of her when he pulled it over his head, let the material slide down his back? Or was it just blindly pinched from a drawer in the morning dark of his bedroom? Did Corner Girl understand the shirt had come from Emma, that it meant something to him? Or was it something he wore when he knew he might get grotty? In the T-shirt, despite the new lines around his eyes and the patina of time across his face, she could almost see the Michael she used to know. The other night, with the White Stripes playing, that old Michael was there. As if time had folded over itself and for that moment, the years hadn't passed at all.

But they had. And there *was* a Corner Girl. His reaction seemed to underline that. So why did she care at all? She just didn't want to be in an argument with him, she told herself. They'd wasted so much time. At least there should be some truth surrounding the pyre that was their relationship. And now she couldn't for the life of her understand what his intentions were. If he was in a relationship, what in the world was he doing getting her all desperate for him again? She wasn't. But she was.

What did any of this matter? It was too late. But then why had he contacted her? Why had he come to her house smelling and looking so good, bringing up old times like they'd been on his mind? She should write the whole thing off, but if there was one thing she knew about Michael, it was that he was pure at heart, he was a person of honor. And so it wasn't easy to write off the whole thing as a man cheating on his wife, looking to fill his hole with the one who got away and then get back to taking out the rubbish. Despite how very clearly it did look that way.

So she clicked. And clicked some more. In his timeline photos, When Michael was dressed fancy, and there was a date stamp, but no information about the event, she wondered: was this his wedding? Was it someone else's wedding? Again, no women grasping onto him in the photos. Strange, right? Had this been recently edited, or had there never been anyone after all? Was Corner Girl a complicated story that amounted to nothing significant—except in her mind?

She saw a novel that he had posted a glowing, to-the-point review about. She clicked straight through to Amazon. Her copy of *He Did the Right Thing* would arrive in two days' time. It didn't have many reviews, but the ones it did have were incredible. She bought it. This in itself was so satisfying, it brought her back to the deliciousness of the days before she'd clicked ACCEPT, when her imagination steered the whole endeavor: Was he into *Game of Thrones* like everyone else? *She* never got it.

She found a comment on one of his friend's posts that said, "Loser," where he'd created a fancy gif about the upcoming GOT episode. She was willing to overlook that discrepancy. Even husbands and wives enjoyed separate interests. On the other hand, maybe she had judged GOT too harshly because of all the gratuitous, raunchy on-screen sex that had forced her to shut her blinds in case a neighbor thought she was getting off on pornography. At least with Outlander there was romance, love, passion. And of course, Jamie.

But this was different from the free roaming along the photographic history of Michael's life, she'd enjoyed before she'd accepted his friendship request. Back then she wore a protective layer of superiority because he'd requested a friendship with *her,* and she'd not accepted. But now she had, and the field was level, all armor off. And Corner Girl was real. Like it or not.

. . .

IN THE CAR, the matcha latte was too hot to drink. The first sip burned her tongue. The radio was playing nonstop ads and she didn't have the patience to scroll through her podcasts. Silence was best. Immediately, her thoughts returned to last night. After the Facebook stalking (what else could she call it?), she'd climbed up a stepladder to the top of her closet to pull down her old photo albums. Maybe she could find something that could tell her a little bit more about how things really were between them. People often said her eyes gave her away, and looking at her gaze peeking out from inside the crook of Michael's arm on some random beach day, beers in hand, she could see why they'd said it. She had a watery, glazed look that could only translate as far gone, the kind of intense love that made everything fade away in comparison. But surely that was a result of their youth, hormones.

She had stared at that version of Emma and Michael until her eyes blurred and her head ached. But she couldn't fully rationalize away that love in her eyes, in his eyes, too, for that matter. Why was she so intent on doing so when she was so angry at him and when he had Corner Girl and God knows who else back in Boston? Why was she so desperately trying to stop herself from pulling down Michael's school sweatshirt that was hiding behind the photo albums, and burying her face in it?

Because if she'd been wrong about the reasons things hadn't worked out with her and Michael, then her whole life—the one she'd made for herself so proudly, as an adult—was a pile of bull honkey. And because, despite appearances, deep down she trusted Michael and felt her instincts lean toward the benefit of the doubt. But, wrong seemed to be her middle name right now. What did she know?

She'd gone through all the greatest photographic hits: high

school graduation, the prom, her first day at university, the day Michael's youngest cousin was born. She remembered them laughing at the name that the parents had picked, one of those unconventionally spelled, impossible to live up to names like: Wynner or Destinee, she couldn't remember which. But she could recall how they'd almost broken into laughter when she'd said it for the first time in front of the new parents. Michael had squeezed her hand to stop her. She hadn't dared look at him until the urge had passed.

Emma searched diligently to find a shot that reminded her of the bad times, but aside from stupid arguments about who was better at navigating maps and misplaced anger that was simply caused by missing each other, she couldn't find anything. Until she got to the Paris photos.

He featured in only one of them, and there was a stiffness to his posture she didn't remember. It wasn't too different from how he'd looked the other night, walking off along the Kailua shoreline. She didn't know what to think. How had it all gone so wrong? And why did it suddenly matter so much? Wasn't she past all of this? And even worse, what if *he* only cared for posterity's sake? A married man, if that's what he was, wouldn't be able to switch paths and fix things now. He probably had no desire to.

She should send him a message. Find out once and for all. Maybe even apologize for not realizing what he'd been trying to do for her all those years ago, misguided as he'd been.

But not yet. And that caveat had held her back from doing so all week, during which she perfected her D.N.E. presentation and tried to pretend like she wasn't online stalking her ex-boyfriend. And of course like it wasn't having any affect on her whatsoever.

Suddenly it was Sunday, when she usually made her beautiful walnut cranberry pancakes. And that was a highlight of her week. And she wasn't going to let that fall to the wayside, along with the comfy blanket and nightshirt just because she'd let so many other things go this week.

Shaking out the laptop neck she'd gotten from craning over the keyboard, and slapping the screen shut, she'd made her way to the kitchen, gathering the bowls and scraper, fork and spatula, convincing herself she was already feeling better.

Emma measured out the dry ingredients, but when she looked for the egg carton, she remembered she'd run out two days before when she'd made an omelet for dinner. Could that really be? She never ran out of anything. She was self-sufficient. She was a Taylor, for God's sake! And Taylors were always prepared for any eventuality. She kept Meals, Ready-to-Eat packed with a first aid kit and a five-gallon jug of clean drinking water, after all. It was the gift her father had given her when she moved to Oahu, and thankfully, except for the one time there was a false alarm missile alert, she'd never had to touch it. And even when she had, she'd been inappropriately delighted at how prepared she was, how she went down to her building's cellar with all those items and sat down calmly while everyone else ran around panicking. She didn't think about how her father would be proud of her, because he wouldn't. He would just say something like, "Of course. That's what you do in that situation."

It was time to reach out to Michael. But instead, she found herself texting Candace to see if she could meet for brunch.

Candace: Wish I could. So not having a good morning already. Would love to go to The Waffle Iron and hear you try not to talk about how bad you have it for Michael. We'll go for lunch on Monday instead: red velvet pancakes with whipped cream? I'll book a table.

At least there was that to look forward to this afternoon. As she pulled into the carpark, Emma felt a welcoming thrill at her final picks for the celebrity and art contest parameters and judges. Things weren't all bad, she had to remind herself. Success at work and whipped cream.

She emailed her report to Sarah and caught up on some administrative tasks, and by noon she was at The Waffle Iron, a place known for indulgence, which was exactly what she was after.

"So, what was going on with you yesterday?" Emma asked.

"The kids were just cranky. I think Ellie has been crying for a month straight."

"Why?"

"Oh, I don't know. Something to do with... everything?"

"Maybe I can babysit the kids and you and Tom can go and have a night out."

"That would be awesome. Let's do it. Next Saturday?"

"Sure."

"I can always count on you, can't I?"

"Yeah, o'course."

"So, what happened with Michael?"

Emma went through the evening in the kind of excruciating detail she herself despised, but she couldn't seem to help herself. It was as if she thought that if she could recreate exactly what had happened then she could fix it, change the ending—like in *Romeo and Juliet*, when she kept thinking, *Just shut up, Romeo, and then you'll both survive.* She knew then and now that it was impossible. What she needed was to look forward.

"When did you say was the last time you spoke to him before all this?"

"Oh god. It was back when I first came home from Paris, for my dad's promotion ceremony."

"Oh, I remember that. The black eyeliner."

"I'm pretty good at that."

"Sure, but you didn't have to wear it, to say, the supermarket. The scarves were good. I'll give you the scarves." Candace paused. "I remember what happened. You hid from him in the supermarket—with your eyeliner—"

"And my scarf."

"And your scarf. Must have been a magical scarf, because it made you disappear behind the—what was it?"

"Vienna Sausages."

"Ah, yes. Canned wieners."

"Yup, that was close." When she thought about it now, it was as if it had happened yesterday. The memory had all the excitement of the *new* them, but with a desperate shadow overlay, like they both knew that was going to be the end of them. Which it was.

"Yeah. Imagine if he actually saw you. Who knows what could have happened? Well, that's a pretty long time ago. What has it been? Ten years?"

"Eleven." Emma said before she realized how desperate that had come across. At least she'd left off *and three months*.

"Can I be sentimental here in a way I know you don't usually appreciate? Candace smoothed back her hair into the lumpy bun, which was unusually messy. The finger combing had hoisted a section into a ridiculous sticky-uppy loop that Emma tried to gaze at so Candace would get the hint.

"Permission granted."

"Do you think it's possible that you still love him?"

"*No!* Stop."

"Do you?" Emma was happy to let Candace walk out with the ridiculous hair now.

"What *is* love, anyway? You know where I stand on all of this. It's messy and it's too hard and, you know, random. It's not necessary. If it happens, great, if it doesn't, well, that's fine, too. I don't *need* anyone." Her words were tripping over one another, though she told herself to slow down.

"Yes, I know. You're the strongest person in the world. You don't need anyone. Your family lives all the way in Italy, you've lived all over the country, all over the world, and you came back here because you like it and it seemed like a homey place when you were here the last time."

Quite hostile, crazy hair lady. "And *you're* here."

"Well, of course. And here you stayed. You're not sentimental at all."

"Your hair's a mess." Emma exhaled. Let that be her response. She wasn't sentimental. She just liked living on Oahu. She liked complaining about the traffic even though she travelled the wrong way and didn't really get stuck in it. She secretly liked the Spam musubi. And she loved the fact that she could get out and swim in the ocean every single day if she felt like it. There was also the rain—how she could tell exactly when it was going to stop and when it would really stick in. She liked both of those. It suited her. Kailua was imperfect, disorganized, but even the lack of parking seemed to work out in her favor: someone always pulled out just when she needed a space. It fit. Even down to the bit where she got to say she lived "on" a place instead of in it, like everyone else.

Paris was sophisticated and new all the time, but new got old after a while. Though she'd never admit that, she could sense the action of moving back had spoken for itself. She chose to ignore that fact and deny it if it ever came up. Had she done the same with the dominance of Michael in the memories that made Kailua so homey? Was every word that came out of her mouth complete bullshit?

"Have you even gone on a holiday since you've been back?" Candace continued.

"Hawaii is a holiday."

"Right. Just think about it." Candace lifted her phone to

check the time and stretched her back like she was preparing to go.

"Whatevs. What does that have to do with anything?"

"I just think you can sometimes suffer a little tunnel vision." Emma picked up the check and reached for her wallet.

"Tunnel vision? I'll try not to take that personally while I pay for your lunch."

"Listen, I'm your friend. I'm not your compliment machine. And thanks for lunch, by the way. Every little bit helps."

"A compliment machine. Now that is a great creative idea. And you're welcome," Emma said. They both stood and reached for their handbags.

"Sure, sure. So, you need to reach out to him and find out what's going on. Once and for all. You both played parts in the end of your relationship. Perhaps it's time to work out if that was a mistake." Candace finally pulled the elastic from her hair and re-fastened the lump, slightly less lumpier this time.

"Aren't you meant to be warning me of the dangers of going back?" Emma thought at least Candace would yank her back from going off the brink.

"It is dangerous. That's true. But I don't think you'll ever be able to move forward—either with or without Michael—before you work out what you both wanted back then, and what you truly want now."

She was right. It was annoying how people outside of a situation could have so much perspective. As if they could step into your shoes and fix everything in two seconds, while you yourself would only make a ridiculous mess of things.

But her lumpy-haired friend didn't know about Corner Girl. Emma was quite positive Candace would have a different take if she did. So why didn't Emma speak up?

Instead she handed the check and debit card to the cashier. "*Mahalo*," the woman with hair down to her knees said, clearly not meaning it as she waited for Emma's receipt to inch through the slot, and then reached for the next person's cash. Emma wouldn't let one unfriendly woman rattle the bond she had with her home. Would she?

In the car, Candace brought the conversation back to D.N.E. "Now it's my turn to ask a favor. Just remember to stay on message with the agreed-upon pitch when the client comes in next week. I know you've been positioned for a new creative role, but the business side of this thing still pays the bills. And that's my forte."

"Of course," Emma said, though she wasn't sure she liked Candace's tone. Was her friend unhappy about the role Sarah had presented to her? Mingled in with the lumpy hair, something about Candace was definitely off.

ELEVEN

EMMA

Emma typed the message in her car, right before she started the drive home.

Sorry about the other night.

Hell no. She wasn't sorry. She tried again.

I don't like how we left things the other night.

Best to stick with straight talk and leave out dramatic superlatives at times like this. Being *really, really* sorry wasn't going to win her any points.

Perhaps we both have some questions and things we'd like to say?

She hit SEND and felt better already. Proactivity had its own propulsion.

Emma turned left onto Ala Moana Boulevard and used her hands-free steering wheel controls to scroll to her mother's landline number in Italy. She picked up on the second ring.

"*Ciao.*"

She tried not to roll her eyes. Why shouldn't her mother immerse herself in the local culture? Wasn't that what she herself had done in Paris? *O-ui.* She'd nailed the inflection. Taken some heat at home for it, too. But the essence of a place seduced her, seeped into her. It was all part of the immersion and, in her experience, it was useless to try to hold back.

"So, Mom, I was thinking of coming out. To Italy. Time for a holiday, don't you think?" In truth, Thanksgiving was rapidly approaching, and she had hoped her parents would call her first this year, beg her to come. But that wasn't their style. Her "hoping" was the definition of insanity itself. Mom and Dad didn't go in for putting pressure on. They'd grown up with too much of that—guilt-laden phone calls from Emma's grandparents that covered nothing so much as how long it had been since their children had phoned, outright anger over holidays spent with the in-laws instead.

"Oh, honey, that is so lovely. We have just made the guest room livable."

Not Emma's room, the *guest* room. She was thirty years old and should really get over it. Not everyone had their very own bedroom in their parents' house. In fact, most probably didn't. But her parents could afford to. And if they understood her better, they'd see how important such a thing was to her. And they'd indulge it, no matter how childish. She secretly wished they'd see through her steely façade, because isn't that the kind of magical connection parents are meant to have with their children?

"We've removed all the poisonous materials, all the dangerous stones that were falling out. You'll love it."

"Wow, that sounds really homey, Mom."

"I know, I know. But you will. You'll love it. These old villas are gorgeous. There are these charming old pigeonnier cutout windows, and we ordered this beautiful bed from the lady next door who's dying."

"She's not dead, and she sold you her bed already?"

"Yeah, yeah. People do it here all the time." Her mother was always applying her own experience to local populations in general. It was something that drove Emma nuts, but also made her laugh: wouldn't someone so worldly realize how bizarre that was?

"Really?"

"Really. It's just a thing. It doesn't mean anything."

Boy, who does she sound like? Emma was starting to think that maybe she herself wasn't as switched onto her own behaviors as she suspected. "You can have tunnel vision," Candace said. Is it possible that Michael, the one who had once known her best, *had* known her better than herself? How disturbing was that possibility?

"How's Dad?"

"You know your dad. He's always a curmudgeon. 'All the Italians are so great. If only they weren't Italian.'"

"Yeah, I bet he's got a big belly from all those Italians cooking pasta."

"He would, but would you believe he's started walking? He walks for, like, three hours every day."

"Dad's doing that?" He'd been fit during all his years of service, but when he hadn't made the promotion list as an o7 Brigadier General, he'd hit a wall, packed on the pounds and left the army disillusioned. His whole family had dedicated their lives to service, he'd been tops on everything, but a handful of people had decided that was the end for him. It wasn't personal. It was the way things worked, and he'd kept up a good show of being absolutely accepting of everything, knowing this was coming one day, but Emma could tell it had taken a toll on him.

Her parents had done the RV thing for a while, considering the various low retirement-tax states, before settling in Italy on a romantic whim. Her mother had always dreamed of returning to Italy. She'd loved their posting there. In fact, Emma had been conceived there. However, she doubted the Italy of today's reality would live up to her mother's intellectualized version. But her father understood the sacrifices Emma's mother had made for his career. And if Italy was what she wanted now, he'd embrace that. They were a team. And it was his turn to take a punt. That was why his new lease on life she was hearing about was a surprise.

"Loves it. There's a beautiful mountain road here. I'm sure he'll take you."

"Okay, sounds good." She pictured the two of them on a mountain, but the image was at least fifteen years out of date.

"I'm gonna go, honey. And you book those tickets for any time that suits you. You know we always want to see you."

"Okay, Mom."

"*Ciao.*"

I love you, too.

Once she was back home and on her laptop, she checked her Facebook notifications. Instead of a reply from Michael, she'd received a notification from him with a calendar alongside it.

Thanksgiving brahs!

She clicked and saw a Facebook event for that Friday evening, an inexplicable five days before Thanksgiving. She'd always loved-hated the *brah* thing, but it grew so densely around her that she had long ceased fighting it. Just the opposite, it had become a Michael thing—and a Michael thing so genuinely meant, unless, of course, it was being used as a four-letter word —that she grew to love it.

Mark your calendars! I'm in Hawaii and want to have a beer with all of my favorite people after we've digested our meals.

That was the day she was meant to fly to her parents.

So what? If she was still one of his favorite people, why

didn't he want to answer her question and in place of doing so, invite her to a group event where he wouldn't have a chance of talking things over? Because he was a man. She could speak man. At least she could try.

She shouldn't see him again anyway. It was just a little fantasy. She'd indulged, and now she'd only reinforced the argument that returning to exes was bad.

Still, she watched the comments pouring in and repeatedly refreshed her phone's Google browser. It occurred to her that she could comment, too. What she really wanted to ask was why he was only reaching out to his friends now? He'd been on island for a while. Of course, that was off limits.

James: Hey Brah! I'll be there. Hope this time you might staying out past 10.

Corey: Aloha! Mai tai will be waiting for you.

And then, words from the man himself:

Michael: James, that was one time, and I had the flu and had worked twelve days straight. Corey, better make that a double.

Corey: Yeah, you need it, brah! A double for me, too.

Why did he *need* it? Surely, he wouldn't have shared about his encounter with Emma. He wasn't that kind of guy. Even the first time they'd started dating, nobody had known for months. He liked to keep important things to himself.

Which is probably why Corner Girl doesn't get any Facebook shots.

If she was going to see him again, she was going to have to ask the serious questions. And if he didn't want to answer them, well, that would be that. Again.

No. She would be safely en route to Italy instead. She closed her eyes, drew two deep breaths, and tried to think clearly, unemotionally. That was the right thing to do, wasn't it? Forget the whole thing once and for all. For real this time. She'd given it a shot, and things had gotten ugly. Again. For all she knew, he hadn't realized she was on the invite list for drinks night. He probably had all his Oahu contacts in one group and hit *SEND*.

Still, eyes closed, breathing deeply, her mind wandered: Did those guys come home every year? How had she managed to miss that? Why did she care?

Because it was fun with Michael, and his crew, and everything around Michael and his crew. It had always been fun, and that's why she'd come back here. *Really, really* that was why. For fun. The kinds she hadn't had in Paris. And while she was already doing the honesty thing, save for a night or two with Candace here or there, she might be comfortable in her home, but she wasn't having all that much *fun*.

The concentrated deep breathing hadn't brought any concrete answers, and Emma took that as a sign to go ahead with her Italy plans despite what Candace had advised, despite the words she wanted to get out. She was looking for some kind of emotional confirmation that Italy, not drinks with the brahs was the right move, but again, nothing.

She was playing it safe. And that was another thing Taylors were very proud of. They'd be the last people on earth when the apocalypse came. *But would it be fun?* The thought popped up of its own accord, but she ignored it. *Fun isn't everything.* Isn't it? "You'll be alive," her father would say. Safe. And for the first time, this argument clearly didn't stand up. Why, suddenly, did *fun* seem so important? When she'd still pictured a future with Michael, she'd pictured lots of fun —two or three little kiddies, playing dumb board games with complex rules amidst uncontrollable gales of laughter. *Of course, there'd be poop, too, Candace*, but no one pictured that, obviously.

Still, she could have fun on her own. She just had to try new things: paddle boarding, acapella singing (did people still do that?), making hand-churned ice cream or her own sourdough starter.

Unconvincing as those ideas were, she typed in *flights from Honolulu to Florence* and waited for the screen to populate. Three hours later her flight was booked. The only flights left at that late date were the day after Thanksgiving. Literally nothing in the six days leading up to it, when she'd have off from work. Her parents wouldn't be upset about it; they just didn't have it in them. They might hassle her for poor planning. But they'd eat their turkey the next day. What was the big deal? Things like specific dates didn't bother military families, who were often apart on birthdays (even the very first one, in her case). But now she would be here during the night of Michael's drinks do. And she feared she wouldn't be able to bring herself to miss it.

TWELVE

EMMA

"Good morning, everyone!" Emma turned to Candace. It was Tuesday. Three days until the big D.N.E. meeting. "Got you a pumpkin spice latte. It's officially that time of year! I know you love it."

"You read me like a book." Why did Candace still seem slightly peeved?

"Yup. I'm pretty much perfect."

"So, guess whose plan has already been approved for a five-person team as long as we get the go-ahead at the D.N.E. meeting?"

"Yours. Congratulations. It's not like this ever happened to you before." Emma stopped short of sticking out her tongue, which she was proud of.

Candace was being weird, this following her comment the other day warning Emma to "stay on message" during the D.N.E. pitch and insinuating that it was Candace's role, not Emma's that paid the bills.

"Well, third time's a charm, isn't it?" said Candace. "Maybe this time I'll get that big promotion: VP! Don't you want higher-ups in your pocket when you're off being all wooh-wooh creative?"

Ouch. "When you put it that way, I guess so. Just call me Jared Kushner."

"You know what's lovely? How happy you always are for me."

That barb wasn't even veiled. What exactly was going on here? Emma would like to show her friend where she could stick that pumpkin spice latte. Now wasn't the time, but she'd have to get to the bottom of it.

"*You* know what's lovely?" Emma said.

"Are you about to get real with me?"

"No. Was just going to say it's lovely that they still sell coffee that's just coffee. Pretty soon, I probably won't be able to get it. Maybe I should stock up." *Yes, Emma, that's the way to make your point: insult her beverage choice. Score!*

"That's just the Parisian in you. I forgive you. Besides, aren't you currently addicted to green tea?" Were they pointing out each other's hypocritical tendencies now? Didn't Candace have Matt for that? It didn't seem like Emma would be able to ignore the tension between them for much longer.

"Not asking for forgiveness." Emma couldn't help herself; she'd picked up on the vibe. She'd regret it, certainly, but at the moment her word choice seemed out of her hands. Confrontation was about to become her middle name.

"You're a dying breed, Emma. You're going to have to face it."

"What's that supposed to mean? This world is headed for one big toasted chai almond milk pumpkin latte with a peppermint swirl. And you've got to be in it to win it? Why should I?"

"Nobody's telling you what to do, Emma. You're a big girl."

"Thank you for explaining that to me."

"You're welcome."

They both looked at each other for a moment; if Candace's thoughts were anything like Emma's, she was wondering what the fuck was going on with them.

"Anyway, I've got some work that's right up your alley. The kind of thing you can bring into your office, close the door, and do all by yourself."

"Lovely." Emma said the word like a curse. But Candace was right. She was a big, un-fun loner. That finally decided it. She was going to Michael's Thanksgiving drinks. But she certainly wasn't about to share that with Candace at the moment.

On Tuesdays Emma and Candace usually made a habit of bringing a picnic lunch to the harbor across the road to watch the cruise ships unload thousands of tourists about to get an earful of *aloha* and a bellyful of kalua pork. It was fun to try to work out where they came from and when they'd pull a photo *shaka*.

But that day, Emma had been by herself under their usual shady palm (the only shady palm). Following the tense interaction, it seemed to be a given that they wouldn't be lunching together. She clicked on the event on her Facebook app and hit *Going*.

LATER THAT AFTERNOON, Candace sent a message asking if Emma would be in town for Thanksgiving. Was this an apology?

Come to my house for Thanksgiving. My kids love you. Especially when you keep giving them all that cash. Why do you keep giving them all that cash anyway? At last count Georgia had $150 stuffed inside Peppa Pig's dress.

She wasn't exactly saying *she* loved Emma, but it was generous, given the mood between them. More than Emma would have been capable of, certainly.

You've got to have money. Just in case.
Coming?
Sure. Why not?

Her response wasn't overflowing with love-hearts either, but at least they were on the right track. And further alienating someone else she cared for wasn't something she was eager to do anytime soon.

THIRTEEN

EMMA

The next morning there was a message in her in-box. Before the alert faded, she could tell it wasn't from Mr. Tea, but Mr. Old Flame himself. She didn't click. Yet. She was awash in some kind of uncontrollable excitement.

It was like she was fifteen again. Her stomach plummeted and her chest swirled in anticipation. It was like a delicious little treat waiting for her. I won't even touch it until I get to work, she told herself. *Enjoy the anticipation a bit.* Besides, she remembered the regret following her acceptance to the drinks invite, and she was certain that was the kind of thing, or worse, that would follow reading the message. In the meanwhile, she could imagine it said anything she liked. And she was surprised to find how open she was to that idea, as if the anger would not exactly disappear, but make way with open arms for Michael, if he said the right things.

On the way out of her apartment, she tripped on her Amazon padded envelope containing *He Did the Right Thing*. Emma slipped it into her tote bag and made for her car.

She considered it something of a feat to have made it to 10:00 a.m. before clicking on the message notification.

I'm glad you're coming to drinks at La Mariana.

Why was she smiling so hugely? It wasn't an apology. It wasn't an admission of anything. She had been spending so much time with his online presence, she was becoming the queen of reading between his lines. Most likely, she was reading too much into the white spaces, but even if she told herself she wasn't serious about any of it, she knew it wasn't true.

She wouldn't answer right away. Let *him* wait for *her*.

On the way home from work, she passed by Kaka'ako. She noticed a whole new strip of stores behind the SALT complex she'd been to the other night with Candace. To have missed this meant she hadn't even driven down that street in years. Which meant she was doing the same old thing each and every day. Now, wasn't that the definition of fun, Emma? There were a couple of cute, trendy-looking cafes, restaurants, and boutiques. She pulled into the high-rise parking structure and made a beeline to Mr. Tea. She was going to do something fun right that very minute.

Inside Mr. Tea Emma was slightly baffled by the menu, but the hipster behind the counter asked her which flavor of tea she liked, what kind of milk, and then said he'd make her something awesome. In a few moments her name was called, and the hipster handed her a foil-sealed cup with a fat straw she was meant to poke through the top. On her first sip, the giant straw sucked up a chewy tapioca pearl and she bit into the novel texture, skeptically, but found the flavor spurt surprisingly pleasant. She looked around. Everyone was on a computer, iPad, or phone. She tried her best not to fall into an us-vs-them mindset while she pulled out *He Did the Right Thing*. The tapioca pearls slid into her mouth, and she allowed her tongue to explore their tacky texture. She liked them.

The book was slow to start—dense language in a heavy tone that made her feel like she was wading in mud. After three pages, she looked up. There was a guy, short, wearing an old surf T-shirt, sucking on a big straw like she was. It couldn't be. But it was. Corey—Michael's best friend from high school, with whom she'd never quite hit it off. She'd seen his comments on the homecoming drinks post about the mai tais, so it was clear they were still in touch. She felt like he could tell she was reading *He Did the Right Thing* because she'd seen Michael's post on it. Though she'd told herself this was just another step in her curious investigation of Michael, she feared it would look a lot like stalking to Corey.

In response, she went steely in self-defense as soon as he laid eyes on her, leaning her elbows on the book. She couldn't help it. That was what she did. Emma felt her face harden into its default stance and in doing so, she didn't even bother sliding the book onto her lap. She knew how to win at stand-offs, how not to look weak. This was what Taylors did.

"How've you been?" she asked, not exactly inviting him over.

"Good," he said, putting one foot out, then hesitating to approach. "You?"

She dipped her chin, still in steel mode. She decided to lower the temperature on her chill slightly. "What are you doing back here?" She tried to smile but was sure it came out as disgusted, or, at best, annoyed. To compensate, she gestured with her palm that he should come sit opposite. He did.

"Settled back here a few years ago." He shrugged.

She saw his ring. "You married?"

"Yeah, you know."

There was a silence in which they both likely thought of Michael—their connective tissue. She would not be the first one to say his name. "How long you here for?"

"Ummm, not quite sure," he said.

"Okay, but you'll be around for Christmas?"

He nodded. "And you?"

She nodded, dragging out the world's most interesting conversation.

"Where you working?" he asked.

She told him all about her marketing firm, Geo Viral.

"Sounds like an STD. A bad one."

"I know." Great. This would be what he'd tell Michael about when he mentioned their meeting. No need to have worried about them getting entangled at all! She quickly moved onto some of the big-name clients, explaining that they loved having a marketing company in Hawaii; it gave them a reason to come, didn't it?

"Never thought about it that way," Corey said.

"Yeah, it can be glamorous sometimes, but mostly it's just sitting at the computer." Why didn't she mention her imminent promotion? Wasn't she supposed to be trying to appear awesome? What was this drivel?

"Tell me about it."

At that moment, Corey's phone rang to the tone of some pop song he should have been embarrassed by. He shrugged. "My daughter picked it," he said, his insta-smile so telling she decided to skip the zinger. "Hang on."

Watching him inspect his phone screen across the table felt familiar. She couldn't quite remember why they disliked each other so much. He pressed the cell's side button to ignore the call. "Just got to send a quick text."

"Okay."

Corey clumsily typed in a note, cursing at the errors. "Damned autocorrect," he said. And then they went back to their stilted conversation.

Five minutes later, Emma was shocked to see Michael stride

through the door. From the tug at his brow and slight bulge of his eyes, an initiate like herself could tell the shock was mutual. He took the least roomy seat—in the small booth next to Emma.

Corey smiled. "Ah, you guys still have it."

She didn't know why he didn't tell her it was Michael on the phone. Why was it so important he gauged their reactions in this double-blind experiment?

Michael looked down at the book. His eyebrows shot up. Amusement. *Fuck.* By now, she actually believed she had been merely reading a random book she'd come across in her Amazon recommendations. Emma was that good at self-deception. In fact, she half-wanted to recommend it to him, because it was full of itself like he was. She was aware her defensive mode colored her assessment in a shade that was not exactly true to life, but she was good at ignoring that.

In the days since she'd felt the wound freshly re-sliced, she'd tried to forget how amazing it had felt to be near Michael that night. But there was no denying it now. As they got used to seeing each other, his eyes welcomed her in like they used to. Like they shared a secret between them. It had always been that way. And it was just what she'd been picturing all these years—when she allowed herself to picture it. How could it still be like this?

He gestured grandly toward the book just as Emma tried to slide it under the table, and she looked at his hand, which did not have a ring on it. Why hadn't she noticed that the last time? Weren't women meant to have built-in homing devices for this kind of thing? Still, it didn't mean he wasn't married.

She looked up and now she noticed him noticing her notice his ring finger.

This was not going well. Still, she wanted to reach out and grab the hand of the ring finger in question. She remembered how, on several occasions, in crowded, loud gatherings, he'd simply grabbed her hand and squeezed—an act that had sent her body humming. It had even once led to them escaping to his car for some very un-Emma-like behavior.

And then, suddenly, he grabbed her hand beneath the table where Corey couldn't see. She flashed to the car memory and then told herself to stop it. Why hadn't anyone spoken in what felt like an unusually long time? What would Corner Girl think?

"I can't believe you're sitting here," Michael said.

"I can't believe *you're* sitting here," she said. Were they pretending they hadn't seen each other last week? And why was she agreeing so readily to be complicit in this?

"Well, you look great," Michael said.

She hated herself for instinctively patting down her hair. Damn you female mating instincts. Damn you to hell.

"Well, thanks," Corey said, as if the compliment were meant for him. "I was beginning to think you guys had forgotten I was here."

"Sorry, brah," Michael said, though he hadn't turned from Emma. "You really do," he said to her. She was in her typical office gear, which in Hawaii was slightly more revealing than elsewhere. Today it was a sundress with a big belt, shorter than she normally liked, but it had looked good on her in the store. When she wore it, she regularly tugged it down. Now she felt like hiking it up. *Stop it. Wild attraction is no reason to go wrecking your life for someone you know damned well has too much power over it.*

"So do you." He did. This second time she was now used to the *texturing*, she guessed you'd call it, around his eyes. It was lovely. If anything, it made him look like more of a safe haven, which set off warning bells in her mind. Especially now that he seemed to be doubling down on the direct approach. Though she wondered why, she could tell he hadn't had much time at the beach since he'd been here, because his skin wasn't tanned. But he had the proof of all his years out there—spots, freckles here and there. He and his friends used to spend so much time surfing, swimming, snorkeling, things she hadn't been doing so much of lately.

The mix of Michael's old and new features reminded her that it had been a long time since she'd known him. And that idea made her hungry to fill in the gaps, like this knowledge of him was something she must be in possession of. Immediately. And yet she couldn't bring herself to ask the simplest question. *Are you married?*

"Well, we were gonna head out to Kailua Beach Park. Why don't you come?" Michael said.

"Me? I'm wearing my work clothes." *And the last time we went there it didn't work out too well.*

"If I know you, you've got a swimsuit in the car."

She'd just been thinking how they didn't know each other anymore, and yet, he was right.

FOURTEEN

EMMA

Twenty minutes later, Emma was walking out of the dingy changing room, sidestepping sandy puddles in a one-piece that suddenly felt too revealing with its keyhole top, lace-up back, and smaller-than-average butt coverage that the local girls preferred.

"You look good," he said, as she approached the place they'd staked out on the sand. The old spot. God, she hadn't been there in ages. Normally, she went to a spot under the trees and worked or read a book. Had she been avoiding this very feeling of deja vu she was experiencing now? She did more swimming than surfing these days and more often than not she wasn't even doing that. Well, now was her chance.

"You look good, too. But I feel like we've already said this." There was no wiping the smile off her face now. If it was anything like his, he'd be reading her loud and clear. In fact, the heat between them seemed to have hiked several dozen degrees with his shirt off and her body-conscious swimsuit.

Corey was already out in the water. She could just make

him out past the break, resting on his board. The water was calm this afternoon. They sat on towels facing it.

"Nice to be home?" Emma asked.

"Yeah, you know." Michael stretched his legs and leaned back to feel the sun on his face.

"I heard about your mom," she said.

"Yeah. Dad's not very good at admitting he needs help, but Jesus, you should have seen how skinny he looked when I got back the other day. It's like he couldn't feed himself without her." He turned to her, squinting beneath the brim of his hat.

"Well, men are lost without women, aren't they?"

"Sure are." Quickly, he changed the conversation. "And what about your parents?"

"They're good. They're good. Living in Italy."

"Oh yeah? I see the European bug is still in your family."

"It is."

"Sorry I upset you the other night."

She didn't like the way he said that, as if it wasn't what he'd done that he was sorry about, but the fact that his bringing it up had damaged her. "I'm not sure that's the way it went down."

"No? How was it then?" Michael sat up and steepled his hands.

"You revealed that you'd made a decision for me without consulting me, which altered the course of both of our lives."

"With your best interests at heart." His hands parted and chopped the air between them.

"God save us from people who mean well." Emma fought the impulse to clench herself into a tight ball. To stop herself, she rubbed at her hands.

"I'm going to say something I don't very often: perhaps I made a mistake. I made a decision for you, for both of us. And it's possible it wasn't the right one. But do you think it's conceivable that there was something about our relationship at the time that was threatening to you?"

She lay back on the towel she'd rolled out and covered her eyes with her arm. Otherwise she was going to look like one tight fist. No matter how uncomfortable, this conversation needed to happen if whatever they were doing here was going to get off the ground. "Yes. I didn't think so then. But I think it's possible that the young Emma loved you so much that she might have taken you for granted, treated you like an extension of herself. And she wasn't exactly sure back then who she was or who she wanted to be. If she's being completely honest, she might not even know now." Yes, it was less excruciating to speak those words without seeing him.

Still, she felt her body shudder from the effort of getting that out. She'd never uttered the words to herself, much less another living person. This was so not what Taylors did. Weaknesses were to be obliterated, not shown the light of day. They were the kind of thing an enemy could use to kill you. And you never knew when someone would turn out to be an enemy.

She felt a shadow eclipse the sunny patch she'd been baking in. She moved her arm away to see and there he was. On his elbow, leaning over her.

Before she could react, he was closer and then his lips were on hers. This time her shudders meant something different. There was that hallucinogenic swirl, just the way she remembered it—more potent for the years of anticipation.

She wanted to do the right thing, interrupt it by asking about Corner Girl, but she couldn't. Her body seemed to have its own agenda. They were out in the open, so there was no tearing of clothes, smashing of bits. Instead, it was a brush, the feel of his erection on her exposed thigh. The idea of what was between them.

She was bombarded all at once with the old mix of feeling

powerful for bringing him to this state, and laughing at herself for being proud of making a healthy male hard. Wow. What an accomplishment.

Still, in the cyclonic whirl of reactions, she could see why she would have pulled away from Michael in France, belittled him, even. Her reliance on him scared the shit out of her. There she was in Paris, trying to make a life for herself, become passionate about post-modernism, and it turned out it was all meaningless slop compared to Michael in his ripped T-shirt and board shorts. While she kissed and tried not to feel, he looked into her with those wet, intense eyes. What the fuck *was* post-modernism again? She could not give a toss. In that moment, she couldn't imagine why she ever had.

It took every ounce of effort to push him off and sit up. His smirk didn't help.

"So, when did you come back?" he said.

"Well, I've been here, let's see, must be ten years now." *Eleven, but who's counting?*

"And?"

"You know what? It's really, really great." Could she say *really* again?

"What's so great about it?"

"You know, the weather and—"

"Weather? That's what you say when you really don't know."

"No, I've got a really great place, you saw it; and it's all mine, backs up on that little canal." *Really, really, really!* "Got my boat."

"You've got a boat? Why didn't you show me?" He said that as if he suspected she was making it up.

"Yeah. Little. It has a paddle, but I like it."

"Well, I'd love to see it."

"I'd like that." She would. In fact, she couldn't remember

the last time she'd used it. Probably had families of geckos and snails tucked up inside by now.

"I'll give you my number and maybe we can work it out." Somehow, they were touching again. Just their knees this time. How had they gotten here?

Suddenly, Corey was at the shoreline. "You guys coming or not?"

Michael stood, held out his hand and pulled her up to standing.

"Emma," he said, his hand still grasping hers—squeezing in that way she always recalled when a thought of him surfaced. Her body reacted as she remembered, stronger maybe. "It's really you."

Then they hopped on their boards and wore their bodies out in the surf.

THE NEXT DAY AT LUNCH, Emma decided she was going to make an effort to thaw things between her and Candace. She'd brought mochi and when they got a few quiet minutes in the office kitchen, she would share with Candace some of the details of what was going on. She knew she'd hurt her friend by keeping this a secret. Candace was a sharer, and that was the key to their friendship. Doubly so since she knew Emma wasn't a sharer, and being the one she chose to share with meant the world to her. Withholding it was like a knife to the heart. Emma knew that. Perhaps she'd used it unkindly as of late. Now it could be a peace offering.

"Guess what?" she said, holding out the pack of Bubba's mango, vanilla, and red bean mochi—all of Candace's favorites.

"You saw Michael." She plucked two mangos, just as Emma suspected she would.

"How could you take this away from me? How did you even

know?" She knew Candace would be pleased with herself for working it out and that's just what Emma wanted for her friend. It was so nice to have this normalcy with her.

"I saw on your Facebook page that you went to Mr. Tea, which I was very surprised to see, because you always make fun of my boba tea."

"Well, I was just trying to get more in touch with the people —for marketing purposes—like you said."

"I'm sure. And then I saw someone you were *friends* with was also there. Someone might have even taken a photo and tagged him. You were in the corner. I could tell from your hair tie.

She pulled it up and showed Emma. It was Michael and Corey, with a corner of her. Both she and Candace could identify her from the hair tie holding up her ponytail, which one of Candace's daughters had given her and she treasured. Was this some kind of crazy game Michael and Corey played together? Keep the girl unidentifiable in the corner of the photo? Then they could never be pegged down. She could draw out that logic thread, couldn't she: tell the girl she didn't want you, she wanted Paris instead, so she questions everything about herself and you hold all the cards. No. She was being paranoid. It was just a crap photo. Corey was an idiot. Too lazy to fix the image. In fact, he probably hadn't noticed her in the frame at all. He was just as dazzled by Michael as anyone. The man had that effect on people. People wanted him for themselves. Which reminded her she should be afraid. Surely, he knew of his power. She didn't think he was the type to abuse it, despite where her mind had just taken her, but sometimes things happened.

So, what was the deal with that marginalized woman in Michael's photos? It was clear from the small gold hoops she wore that it was the same woman. Why was she always like that? For all the beard burn Emma's chin tingled with from his five o'clock shadow, she hadn't found a way to bring it up. Or she hadn't wanted to.

"So? What was it like?" Candace asked.

"It was terrible. Awful, you know just like people say—if you work something up in your imagination too long, the reality can never add up." She shrugged.

"Liar."

"I know. Why do people say that? Regardless, I've decided I'm not interested." Emma lowered her eyes, like that was the end of that.

"I'm sure you're not. Playing it cool, huh? How's that going?" Candace was leaning in. Was her friend back? Emma hoped so.

"Well, I told him I was really happy with my life, and he seemed to believe me."

"Why? It's not true? What about the nightgown, the blankie? You love your cozy old lady life. You just gave me that spiel the other night at Kaka'ako."

Emma's Spidey sense peaked. "Do you know something about that?"

"About what?"

"Never mind." Now she was being paranoid, suspicious. Surely Candace wasn't sabotaging Emma's cozy existence to prove some kind of a point. That was too far. Even for her. Candace was her closest friend. Sure, they were having some tensions, but wasn't that normal when two red-blooded women were as close as they were?

"But you saw him at the beach? With no shirt on? Fuck, if Matt had one-tenth of the chest that man has . . ."

"You're not really helping."

Now that she was with Candace, sideswiped by disturbing thoughts about her friend's capacity for meddling, she didn't want to share what had happened, nor her concerns about it.

She knew she should if she wanted to fix whatever this was between them. But everything felt too raw and unclassifiable. She wasn't ready to pin it down like Candace would do. While Emma tended to go for the circular, feel-it-out route, Candace had a bull's-eye accuracy that led her straight to the target. And Emma wasn't ready for that.

"Bit of a fan, are we?" Emma raised her brows.

"Look who's talking," Candace rolled her eyes. "But you're better at distancing yourself than I am."

Emma's shoulders bounced. "True." Candace's comment was strangely on the nose, but on the nose of exactly what, Emma couldn't say. "I don't really want to talk about it anymore. Okay?" That was enough effort. A bit of a failure, but she couldn't bring herself to fix it now. She wanted to put the kibosh on this conversation even though it was the best one they'd had in a while. It was costing her too much. And if she wasn't imagining it, Candace seemed to be getting off on that. That couldn't be right and yet...

"Okay, let's change the topic then." Candace raised her palms in surrender and began to talk about Thanksgiving dinner and a few things Emma should bring. She pretended to listen.

"One more thing, though," Candace said, changing courses. "Let's be serious for a second. He's in a relationship. That's what his status says: *Married*."

But Michael's relationship status hadn't been visible. She'd checked. More than once. Had this just been posted? Did it have anything to do with their kiss on the beach the other day? Was that why he'd been silent after their argument? No, that wouldn't be it. The world did not revolve around her. This was too much reading between the lines is all.

"He didn't have a ring on. But who knows? What... what would you do?" Emma tried desperately to seem like the words hadn't affected her, like it wasn't obvious she could barely speak. Could things ever work out between them now?

"You can't mess with married men. The question is: why update the status now? Maybe he's signaling you?" Candace proposed.

Just what she needed, another voice mimicking the same ridiculous worry she'd been harboring. Emma shrugged, but avoided eye contact. "It's probably not smart, but I was thinking maybe he and I can get it out of our system and then go back to where we were. But now I know he's married, I don't know what to think. The thing is he's an honorable guy. It's easy to misinterpret stuff on social media. I feel like we've come this far. I need to at least give him the benefit of the doubt. Surely there's a reasonable explanation? I need to hear him out. Likely, it was just a dumb fantasy of mine—maybe his, too, and after his drinks night, that will be the end of it." Lies, lies, lies.

"Let me get this straight: you spent ten years getting over him, and now your plan is to spend ten minutes throwing all that away just to start getting over him again? Something doesn't add up. You were not hoping to 'get him out of your system.' That is complete bullshit. Can't you be honest with yourself?"

Eleven years. Emma breathed deeply, dropping onto a napkin the mochi she was about to take a bite of. She wasn't going to take the bait. She was sure whatever was motivating Candace's provocation, it wasn't only about this. "It better be more than ten minutes. No, this is a blessing, this status update. I'll save myself a heap of trouble. I don't want to be in a relationship with him. I don't want to be in a relationship with anyone. I don't want to be the unrecognizable woman in the corner of the photo." At least that last bit was true.

"What?" Candace took the last mango mochi as she posed the question.

"Didn't you see, on his page? You can't even make out who the girl is in those photos. And now it looks like that's his wife."

"No, I didn't see that. Everyone is egomaniacal on Facebook. That's the whole point. You can show yourself, and the world, how great *you* are."

"I don't get it," Emma said. "And I don't think Michael is like that."

"With that body? He should be. Seriously, though. Do you honestly believe this would be just a get-it-out-of-your-system hook-up for him? *Especially* if he's married?"

"I really do. I don't think either of us wants to go back there for anything." *Why not? Did she really think Candace was buying this? If he was married, she would, she would. . . oh, what could she possibly do about it? Nothing.*

Now it was Candace's turn to let something go. Emma could picture her friend lasso the words of her disbelief as they tried to make their way from her lips. Instead she reached for humor. "You sure you don't want me to come over and play interference? I'd be good at it."

"I'm sure you would, but I'm a big girl. I can take care of myself. Believe me." *If I can't, someone should.*

After, they hugged their goodbyes in the parking lot, which felt more like them than the fraught tone of their conversation. So much so that she'd almost asked Candace if she knew what was going on between them. But she didn't.

There was too much on her plate trying to figure out things with Michael. Why must everything be figured out? It was exhausting. She could let things sit, unresolved, waiting to see how they naturally unfolded. Couldn't she? Look how she'd been rewarded for that tactic with the relationship status reveal. No matter how difficult, it was time for action.

FIFTEEN

EMMA

It was the hardest Friday morning ever. Mainly because it was really just an extension of Thursday night, as Emma had only managed to fall asleep for ten minutes before her alarm. The blame for that fell squarely on the status she had tried not to look at for four hours, then googled the method of locating, and within seconds saw "Married" under Michael's About section, and spent the rest of the night staring up at the ceiling, vacillating between fury and heartache. The revelation put her feelings into stark clarity: she missed him, she loved him, she always had, and she still wanted a life with him. Even more pathetically, it was probably a main (though, in fairness, subconscious) motivation for her setting up camp here.

By the time the sun rose, she wasn't sure whom she hated more: Michael or herself.

And of course, it was the day Emma was meant to prove herself to Sarah and keep her mouth shut while Candace extolled the wonders of her same-old same-old campaign to D.N.E. There was a lot riding on this: her strained best-friendship, her dream promotion, and her personal proof that she still possessed some element of impulse control.

She woke up late and her outfit was rumpled. She barely had any makeup on. Dragging a brush through her hair and fluffing it up with some mousse, in an attempt to create beach waves, resulted in a grease stain on her blouse that she didn't notice until she sat down at her desk.

"Secret donut?" Candace asked.

"What?"

Candace pointed to the grease. At least her concern would benefit from helping out with said stain. (Women were brilliant, wonderful creatures, but she didn't pretend to understand what motivated any of them—herself included.)

"Happens to me all the time. I had you pegged as a secret bad eater. Like, in front of everyone we're all vego, gluten-free, green smoothies, blah blah, but on a Friday afternoon, Mickey Dee's all the way. Am I right?" She was at the sink, concocting a solution from bottles beneath the sink that Emma had never seen before.

"No. Why would I eat that stuff? Do you know what they put in it?"

"Okay, you pass. I was just testing you. I wouldn't eat it either."

Liar. But she'd let it go. She knew Candace was lying to herself, too. And she was in no place to judge that. "Great. Thanks for that." The stain was gone.

"I take it the status was a shock."

"Remind me again why we're friends?" This love-hate thing was getting ugly. Everything felt like it was right at the surface.

"Do you want me to say a bad word first thing in the morning? Because I'm ready. 'Silly,' 'wackadoodle,' and 'poo-poo head' get old. So don't make me fucking angry." It was impossible to tell if Candace was joking as she waved the cloth she'd used to clean Emma's blouse.

Emma raised her hands in surrender. "Okay, poo-poo head. I'm sorry. But that was quite a wackadoodle bomb." Had Candace *enjoyed* dropping it?

"You're not using 'wackadoodle' right. And you're right. I wasn't very delicate about it."

Why?

"I want to know more, Emma, but we've got to give that presentation to the client today and you've got a very big part in it. We're gonna pull on our big girl pants and do this."

"Of course." But why did it feel like Candace had dropped the bomb at a strategic time? And why did it feel like she was enjoying playing the adulting role here?

Emma's matcha latte had sat so long she was sure it would be cold, but it was still rather hot. It did, however, have a weaker taste than usual. She sat, going over her notes, trying not to see only the word *married* on the pages, sipping mindlessly and cursing Ms. Chloe for giving her a weak tea on such a day. Twenty minutes later, she'd drunk it all and still felt sleepy. Emma fixed herself an awful drip coffee from the pod machine in the kitchen and made her way to the conference room.

A large platter of pastries glistened under the fluorescent lights. The clients brought in a team of six. All were young, wearing slogan T-shirts too cool for Emma to understand, shoe brands she'd never heard of, and masterfully distressed jeans. Not very *aloha*. And yet, they all chanted that over the top Al-O-*ha* that all the tourists get riled up with everywhere she turned. One attempted a *shaka*. One asked if they had coconut milk, and they did; they knew their clients.

She was meant to keep her mouth shut until her part: talking about the illustration art contest and Jimbo Peyton, the skater who'd lost a leg and came back to kill it in The X Games;

he was hot as hell, too. Even hotter because his determination was a fuck-you to weakness.

The art spoke for itself. When she'd stumbled upon illustration as an artform, she recognized right away that it was the perfect category for the contest. The best of it was arresting, covetous, and it was part of everyday life. Anyone could access it anywhere. What an amazing thing to have workaday materials so incredibly adorned, which made us look up from our busy lives, and colored the way we did so.

Emma was suddenly aware that she had been staring at her notes for longer than was normal. People had started to speak but that hadn't bothered her. She didn't look up until Candace kicked her under the table. *Why so tense?* she thought. She took another sip of coffee. She was incredibly focused; her mind was crisp. She was jotting down the perfect articulations of ideas she'd only been able to obtusely skirt around during her preparations. This was going to rock. She was going to blow this out of the water. Normally, coffee made her jittery, but today it was the perfect propulsion toward her sense of purpose.

She may not have wrapped her head around social media, but offline she could read a person right away. It was a skill she'd picked up PCS-ing (army speak for posting out) no less than fifteen times growing up. That was the skill that landed her the job, and most likely it was the fuel for her on-the-pulse creativity. If she wanted to succeed in the task Sarah had set before her, she was going to have to find a way into social media that worked for her. Because that's where the world was going, and if she didn't go with it, she'd be left behind.

Michael popped into her head, and she nearly snorted, but then stopped, because hadn't it worked? She was—not without complications—in contact with him again through social media. It all seemed to click into place. And as for the morality dilemma of it, she was still giving him a chance despite what she'd read about his status. Because she'd been reading between the lines the whole time, and she wasn't going to stop now. She was sure there was a logical explanation. Or maybe she was just telling herself that so she wouldn't feel like a husband stealer. But her mood was so shiny and felt so *right* that in the moment it seemed like *not* trusting him would be the only thing that would trip her up.

Because right then, she flashed to the conversation she and Michael had had before it had all gone so horribly wrong: about how the neighborhood was changing. There was something she could use in that right now in this meeting, and she felt the frisson of excitement she did when an idea began to percolate. There was a bridge; and now she'd found it.

"We have been thinking very hard about what your brand brings to your customer," Candace began, taking the helm in front of the drop-down screen at the head of the oblong table.

"We already know what that is. We bring together all these distinct moieties with their own flavors and cultures to create one uber-moiety that everyone wants to be a part of," said Justin, the head hipster, judging from the volume of his hairstyle.

"Well, first off, kudos to you for being able to bring the word *moiety* into the American vernacular," said Candace in a way that was meant to be complimentary, unless you knew Candace, which Emma did. They'd laughed about how D.N.E. had taken the anthropological term and not only used it improperly, but somehow got the whole world to use it.

Emma abruptly had all eyes on her and she didn't understand why until she looked down to see she was leading her very own slow-clap. She looked down at her hands for a few seconds before she actually stopped. The sound and feel of it was so pleasing to her.

Candace shot her a look. "The only problem now is that you're a victim of your own cleverness. You've created a tsunami of uber-moieties, so that everyone from Oprah to Dora the Explorer has a break-out group of their own now. I heard that social platform moiety.com may overtake facebook in three years' time. So, how do you stand out now?"

Candace knew the pain point of these guys because she did her homework. They were nodding in unison. But Emma herself could see straight down the line of this presentation to one main flaw: their campaign was offering more of the same. Sure, they weren't calling it an uber-moiety, but that was in essence what it was. These guys were going to see through that. Why hadn't Sarah or anyone else? They were so used to copycatting, filling in the templates that no one thought beyond that. And that's why they needed Emma. Change was a'comin' and people like her were going to be steering the tide. Where had this confidence and clarity been her whole life? She felt like she could take over the world.

"We went online and tried to see, in a practical way, how people used to interact with your brand, and how they do now." Candace clicked the remote and her PowerPoint presentation flashed to life. The first graph read, "Number of Times People Have Clicked on an Email from a Brand Five Years Ago, One Year Ago, Last Six Months." The peaks were on a steady decline. The guys exhaled and shifted in their chairs. This was the stuff the higher-ups were hassling them about, no doubt. Cool as Illustration and soon-to-be spokesperson Jimbo Peyton were, they weren't going to reverse the downward trend.

"We can all see the steady decline," Candace said, just to twist the knife. *Make them need you.* It was all on the checklist. "This one is about Facebook interaction; next Twitter; then Instagram." Each slide looked identical. She touched the remote again and the presentation clicked off. Once more and the lights turned on.

"And? What are you saying?" Again, Lion-hair was the mouthpiece.

"People are not interacting with brands online in the way they did before."

"What are you suggesting?"

"We are suggesting going old school. Same platforms you're used to, but with the kind of core celebrities and icons you began with, talking about real things. Doing real things—on Facebook, Twitter, Insta, Snapchat ads, all those spots. We've come up with a four-pronged plan."

Chris was up first, with the inbound segment: Facebook ads to attract the attention of lapsed brand super-fans. Then an email funnel to get them hyped up again with loads of insider-only perks, then exclusive high-end specialty items that the media will be all over, then social media shareables to spread the word and so on.

"Which brings us to the second prong, centered around public relations. Emma—" She palmed her invitation for Emma to stand, but, Emma noticed, she did not sit down the way she had for Chris's speech. Instead, she stood close to Emma.

Emma rose and began to speak. She felt so centered, so comfortable, she didn't even look at her notes. She was aware she was remembering every single point she'd studied, and was as acutely aware that the spiel was not garnering oohs and aahs from the client. It wasn't that the choices she'd made weren't incredible. It was that this was more of the same. They were losing them.

She couldn't quite bring herself to look at Candace, but she knew Candace was feeling it, too. She remembered the things Sarah had said to her, and this overwhelming sense of focus and comfort culminated in her going off script. She heard herself mention, in the ideal way she hadn't been able to articulate the other day, exactly the campaign she'd originally had in mind.

"Number one: Site Install in parks in all the major cities—Seattle, New York, LA, San Francisco, Chicago, Atlanta, Austin, Portland. Make our very own *aloha*-inspired shopping experience right in the park."

"Go on." The hipsters were at the edges of their seats, this time three of them spoke, in unison. Emma had never felt surer of herself.

"You've got Mac Store style check-out, so there's no line. Seamless ease of purchase for buyers to see how you operate, no chance to change their minds; we're not trying to upsell, we're not going tech, we're going old-school personal using all the best tech available to remove any barriers to purchase."

"You mean like hula girls and ukulele music?" Lion-hair was hooked. She could see his knee bounce under the table as his elbows slid wide.

"Emma—" She was aware of Candace speaking, but she couldn't, didn't dare to stop herself. There was a fatefulness to this moment she hadn't considered before.

"Not exactly. What *aloha* really means is personable relationships, caring about those closest to you in the best way." She proceeded to show them a few different types of *shakas*: the blowing up the balloon *shaka*, the mini *shaka*, the flossing *shaka*. Then went on to detail some of the more advanced-funnel spokes of the plan. Guides to walk them through, giveaways, bare feet, plumeria behind ears.

"And they are going to associate these excellent *aloha* feelings with D.N.E. You're even going to make a special plumeria tee-shirt, a few of them, by a series of illustrators whom your audience will choose. Not the gatekeepers, but the buyers themselves." It was the most exhilarated she'd ever been in this office, possibly anywhere in the last decade.

"Emma—" Candace was touching her back now. And not gently. But she kept on.

"Stores like Etsy, they're just climbing the charts while you guys are going backward, and why is that? Because they're creating individual relationships. Nobody wants to go somewhere that treats them just like everyone else. Look at Amazon. They're all about the customer, while making it easy and cheap. But what are you about? What can you bring to the customer that no one else can?

"We're operating in a world where your bank will shut down your card for suspicious activity even if you travel overseas regularly for your job. And then you have to go through a long and painful process to get everything running again. We want our bank to know us. We want them to know we've spent 36 hours traveling to Tokyo and the last thing we need is not to be able to buy a Sapporo in the lounge when we've got an hour between flights."

"Emma; thank you—"

"Yes! Thank you!" shouted the Lion-haired senior hipster. "This is so exactly spot-on."

Emma heard Candace's gasp. She was sorry, but it was all so right, she knew she'd be able to make Candace see that later.

"Sure, we get the security, but we want that to be easy, personable, reasonable, considered, behind the scenes—*aloha*." She heard herself say, "Which brings us to number three: we want you to make a very public message about going off-line.

"Still be available for all those things that people want, but you're taking down your Facebook, Twitter, and you're gonna do it in person, or directly through your website; own your content, own your audience. Bring it all back directly to you." She outlined a few ways they could do so.

"Come on, every company needs to have an online presence today," another hipster said. She should really learn their names. That was unprofessional. The kind of thing Candace had doubtless nailed before she typed a word in their file.

"You already have an online presence. It'll be there until the end of time. It's time to take that into the next phase. We'll walk your customers through it. And we'll get a shed-load of publicity in the process. You'll be the leaders you've always been."

By the end of the meeting, her team had all ceased speaking. Candace had sat down and nodded, maintaining a tight—but, unmistakably to Emma—murderous smile throughout. The client was happy and they signed the papers right then and there.

But the wind had gone out of Emma's sails. She suddenly felt exhausted, as if she needed to lay her head down immediately. She had never experienced anything like this morning's incredible peak of perfection followed by a hollowness so complete she was afraid she might be able to poke right through herself. When she looked up from gathering her papers, everyone had gone.

SIXTEEN

EMMA

Emma was putting the finishing touches on her outfit for the evening. She would put someone's eye out if they accused her of it, but she put a lot of time in getting a beachy wave into her hair, and she was wearing a new dress from one of those expensive shops next to the trendy coffee house, ChadLou's. She decided to splurge on a new lipstick that looked like she wasn't wearing any lipstick, only better, and it was worth it. She looked like a million bucks.

Which was just as well, because she was on her way to the married man she clearly had lots of inarticulate feelings about, and although she'd sealed her new creative position at the company and the client loved her idea, she'd lost her best friend in the process. Looking good was about the only thing going for her at the moment.

Emma could not account for her behavior in that conference room. The clients were obsessed with it. And her boss had called her in to personally thank her for it. She hadn't meant to upstage Candace, but in the moment, she knew she must present her idea, could find no way *not* to, and was equally as positive that the client was going to leave unhappy with the route Candace was taking. If she'd allowed her friend to continue, D.N.E. would have gone to another agency.

Emma had never done anything like that before. She knew when and how to keep her mouth shut. Something had happened—and it scared her. Had she suddenly begun showing symptoms of a dormant bi-polar disorder? Had she been so affected by this Michael thing that she'd lost all hold on reality?

She'd been exhausted when she came home from work and slept for three hours before showering for Michael's drinks event. She felt kind of like she had a hangover now. But she hoped a glass of wine might help that, and it seemed to do the trick. Strange. Almost like she'd been drugged, but all she'd had was that matcha latte, which, if anything, had tasted weaker than usual. She'd been too focused on work for food.

In the Uber, Candace sent her a Facebook message.

You are uninvited to Thanksgiving. I have told Matt and the kids that you are unwell. Which you clearly are.

Candace had avoided her all day after the D.N.E. meeting, which was just as well because Emma had no excuse for her behavior and was at a loss for words. But the un-invitation stung. Was her action completely unforgiveable? She felt terrible and doubted even her glamorous outfit and hairstyle could manage to cover that. The remorse she felt now was so out of sync with the complete clarity to the goal she'd had at the meeting. Something was off. When Emma saw her own behavior in hindsight, what she saw was not admirable.

AS SHE MADE her way around the back of the restaurant, along the pier, with all the expensive boats sleeping beside the docks, she forced herself to compartmentalize. This was a key survival tactic she'd watched her father practice all his life: cancer scare before an international training exercise? Compartmentalize and get on with it. Brother died five days before deployment to Afghanistan? Arrange the funeral, attend, have a final beer, then get on that flight.

She was good at it, too, though she wouldn't want to admit it for fear of what people (like Candace) would read into it. But she was here now, and nothing was going to be fixed with Candace by her screwing up this whatever-it-was with Married —but possibly with an excusable caveat—Michael.

She steered her thoughts on the here and now and touched the profile of the tiki carvings as she did so. There was something solid and reassuring about the ancient wooden gods watching over them. The feel of them beneath her fingers brought her soaring back; it'd always done that. Michael had accused her of being superstitious, which was ridiculous. She just had a thing for tikis. In fact, she had a whole set of glasses like that for the cocktail parties she never had.

Emma closed her eyes, her hand on the wooden sculpture, her face to the ocean breeze and focused: what should she do about Michael? She had to get him out of her system. And she had to trust that he was not a cheater. That there was something complex in play there and that she was not treading on another woman's territory. So this would be one night to lead where it may, and that would be that. She opened her eyes and spun around to enter the open front restaurant.

Speaking of the devil, as she passed the unmanned hostess stand, there Michael was, again with Corey, and Jamie at his other side. Corey nudged Michael, which was pleasing. *He'd been waiting for her.* Emma tried to pretend she hadn't noticed, or couldn't care less if she had.

Of course, she and Michael had shared some intimacy the other day. But the beach towel moment hadn't been followed by a part two and that was probably a blessing, given the whole relationship-status bomb.

Things had gotten a little out of hand. Now they were going in with some distance, some time to have cooled off and think clearly. But from there, it didn't feel any different. In fact, she was stunned by his hand grabbing for hers, that squeeze before he pulled her between his splayed legs on the shabby cane barstool. *He's married.* But she didn't move. She could hear Corey and James, and possibly some others nearby, applauding, and she could smell the beer on his lips, but he touched his nose to hers, and whispered, "I'm so glad you're here."

He didn't look so glad. He looked deadly serious and she hadn't expected that. Perhaps that's what a man looked like when he was about to cheat on his wife.

He pushed into her, like a kiss, but not quite, so that she was now ready to bridge the gap and do it herself because clearly she didn't have a single moral fiber in her body. Shouldn't she be shouldering all moral weight if Michael wasn't up to the task? Despite the shame creeping in, her will to do so was not surfacing. But she did register his friends' eyes on them, and when she heard a hoot, she pulled back. Already she was woozy. There had been no need for the compartmentalizing. Here Michael was, eclipsing everything again.

Corey offered his palm for a complicated handshake she thought he'd have outgrown, and she had a look at his T-shirt: CBD. Central Business District? What was that about? James, whose hairline time hadn't been kind to, embraced her. She was surprise, because as she recalled, he'd never been enthusiastic about communication of any sort. He wore a wedding ring. At least someone still thought it an important thing to do.

· · ·

ALL IT TOOK WAS one piña colada and a couple of old standards done Hawaiian style by the band, which had all of the same members as the last time they'd gathered here, and Emma once again felt Michael's lips on hers. Whatever moral intention she had vanished.

He pulled her onto the dance floor where two other, much older, couples were slow dancing, and she closed her eyes and let the sensations roll over her in beautiful waves. Suddenly, she felt her eyes wet at a thought: was this what it would have been like if they'd stayed together? *Stop it.* And she did. She allowed herself to feel the moment, the past be damned. Corner Girl a.k.a Wife be damned. Tomorrow she could deal with that. But today the answer was clearly to have a mind-blowing night with him and then go their separate ways. That should get this out of their systems and allow them to continue on the messed-up trajectories they'd followed all those years ago, like all the other unhappy people in this world. *But he's married.*

The band took a break and Michael led her back to Corey and James at the barstools. There was a crowd of people from high school there now. Everyone seemed to break out into their longstanding groups and here they were. Minus Candace.

"What's CBD?" Emma asked Corey.

"Oh, here we go," Michael said.

"What?" she asked.

"Corey owns a CBD business right in Kailua."

"What the hell is CBD?"

"Cannabidiol is the oil from marijuana or hemp. The legal stuff. People use the oils, or gummies, or teas, coffees, anything really. Gives you an incredible calm feeling with the benefit of hyper-focus."

Alarm bells went off in her head.

"Does it have a weak taste?"

"Yes, it does, that's why most people mix it with something rich, like coconut milk, or full cream."

She heard James mimic Corey: *full cream*. Michael laughed. But then added, "He's making a killing at it. Needs a marketing team. We're about to work together. Which is probably a huge mistake."

"Wait a minute."

Emma detailed the events of the morning, uncomfortably, but motivated by the hope of a logical explanation. "Do you think Ms. Chloe could have put the CBD in my tea?"

"Chloe from over at Carrot's?" Corey said.

"Yes! Do you know her?"

"One of my best customers."

"I cannot believe it."

Ms. Chloe spiked her tea! She was incredibly angry, but everyone else was laughing, so she tried to smooth her brow.

Michael gave her one of the orgasmic squeezes and she turned to him. "Unethical, if as you say, she gave it to you without asking. But it really isn't anything that will harm you. People take it to sleep, concentrate at work, calm anxiety. And it sounds like you did the right thing at work. The kind of thing you normally wouldn't do because you're too nice. Candace probably knows that, too. She'll forgive you. Whether you should forgive Ms. Chloe, I'm not sure."

"I'm not nice."

"Okay," Michael said.

"And Ms. Chloe probably had good intentions," Corey said. "Fancies herself a bit of a healer."

She enjoyed watching Michael's eyebrow tug even if she guessed the thoughts behind it weren't ones she'd be happy about. *Here's Emma with her crazy healers and drugged tea. Like it was the kind of hijinks she always got into.* When his lips curled into a tight smile, she couldn't help but mirror it. From the shift in his gaze, she could tell he noticed. Their connection was pure instinct. Why had she ever thought she had any control over this?

"And I don't think Candace is going to forgive me. She's uninvited me to Thanksgiving." Now why had she gone and told him that? Because there was no strategy where Michael was concerned. There was just Emma, raw and exposed. This was beginning to feel like Paris all over again because she was unraveling before him. If he noticed, he'd probably get back to his good intentions that ruined everything for them. Or maybe he really had changed. Maybe she had, too. Maybe she could deal with the unraveling now. Maybe that was part of being an adult. Sure. It would all be that simple. Of course it would.

Why not? This was about sating a mutual desire, to finish, as it were, some unfinished business, and then move on with the missing piece slotted in, ready to face life full on. Only partially unraveled, but in the right ways, so that they'd both be open to the right, different people afterward.

Corey and James splintered off from the conversation and they were alone again. Emma switched to Prosecco and by the time she finished off her first split, she was more relaxed. She was going to have a good night, the next day she was going to sleep it off, and then she'd face the consequences of work and a Thanksgiving alone.

Modern Millie was her name tonight: sex and sex only. She could be like that. Why not? After a freshen-up in the toilet and a quick Uber order, she made a bee line to Michael but was cut off by Karen Rodgers. It'd been a blessing that she'd been able to avoid her since living back on island; of course, there were a few close calls, but Emma was a world-class ducker, who now had to pay the piper.

"All those years ago, I heard you and Michael broke up, and then I was so surprised you moved back here! How brave of you." Her expression was pinched in a poor attempt at imitating empathy.

"I wasn't brave at all. It was all part of the plan."

Karen made no attempt to hide her glance at Emma's left hand. "I see you're still single. You're so strong. I admire you for that. I could never be alone. I got married and my husband does everything for me. He's watching the kids now, giving them dinner, putting them to bed."

"Must be nice for you."

"It is. You should friend me on Facebook, so you can see all the photos."

Emma smiled and kept her mouth shut so she wouldn't lie.

"We've got a beautiful place in Lanikai. Even got the private beach key. Kids in private school, holidays three times a year. We're living the life."

"Sounds like it!"

"Should we get a drink?"

"No, I'm gonna go talk to Michael."

"But—"

And there he was again, saving the day. "Now don't hog her all to yourself, Karen! Going to give that Corey a huge thanks for inviting you to drinks! So great to see you, but I haven't seen Emma in ages either, so I'm afraid I'm going to have to steal her away from you."

I forgive you for unravelling me.

They took their seats again. "That was more satisfying than I'd like to admit. Thank you."

"You're welcome."

Emma picked up her phone and started clicking.

"What's so interesting on there?" Michael asked.

"I called an Uber. Would you like to come home with me?" Yes, the direct route was the right way to go. Hopefully she'd be able to keep it up when the topic became more complicated.

"Yes." He sounded deadly serious. *Unravel, unravel.* It was starting to sound strange, meaningless. Certainly not something to be afraid of.

Michael took her hand and led her right past Karen Rodgers, then swung her around so their chests were touching. He leaned in and kissed her. Karen cleared her throat, but Michael pulled Emma right out the door without saying goodbye to his friends—as was his habit.

The Uber arrived and she felt it was probably inappropriate for the blue Hyundai driver named Darryl, who was known for great conversation, to whistle at her, but she enjoyed it, especially in front of Michael, who became instantly protective of her.

"Hey! Par-tay! You guys look like you've been having a great night."

Michael stayed quiet, which was what he did when he disliked someone, but he looked at Emma, pulled her close in the backseat, and began to fondle her hair, as if it was incredibly sexual to him. From what she could see happening in his jeans, it was.

"I have," she said, not taking her eyes off Michael.

"It's the holidays. Everyone wants to be with someone on the holidays. No fun being by yourself."

"You sound like Karen Rodgers! Just because you're not with someone doesn't mean you're by yourself!"

"Karen who? I don't know her, but surely it's better when you're with someone you love, isn't it? Just being honest. You guys know."

They were still looking at each other intently; nothing had changed with those words, but that didn't necessarily mean anything. Silent eye speak was difficult to translate.

That's when she smelled something funny and turned to

notice the incense burner glued to the center console. Darryl was probably on CBD, too.

So that they didn't start giving the CBD dude a Thanksgiving love show he would probably enjoy, she tried to scooch back toward the window and start a safe conversation.

"How are the guys?"

"You know, balding, bored with their marriages, thinking about their secretaries in inappropriate ways. Sounds awesome, doesn't it?"

"No." Emma wondered, if he was married, was that what he did? Is that what *she* was doing here? Fulfilling some kind of outdated fantasy as she'd suspected?

"I think you and I can have a much better talk than I did with those guys."

"Who says I want to talk to you?" Damn her hands at her hair. Didn't she have any self-control?

"Don't you?"

There was no confusing the translation of the silent eye speak between them there. Even Darryl must have understood from the rearview.

BACK IN HER APARTMENT, she pulled out the tiki glasses and whipped up some drinks.

"Two mai tais," she said, handing him one, where he stood by the shelf, looking at her photos.

"Uh-oh, more mai tais? Somebody's looking for trouble."

"Maybe I am."

"Still mad at me?" he said.

"I thought we were sweeping that under the carpet." She was very close and could see Michael's pupils dilate, felt like they were swallowing her up.

"Oh, I didn't get that memo." Michael's chin jutted out and he tipped his tiki glass to take a sip. "Mmmm. Delicious."

"Why Michael, are you trying to flatter me? And yes, you did get that memo. It's written all over my face."

"Well, what if I chose to ignore it?" he asked, his eyes darting to her mouth.

"Still mad at me?" Emma's body was speaking a language of its own. She felt herself lick her lips while she had his attention.

"Nah."

He leaned an elbow on the mantle, and she could see his chest muscles flex beneath his tee shirt. "That must be a very big carpet you've got."

It's going to have to be after tonight. "Shh..."

"Did you just shush me?" Michael asked. His peaked eyebrow twitched.

"Do you want me to shush you?" Oh, she wanted to.

"Is that what the kids are calling it these days?" He smiled. And they were back to that place where she felt there was no way this could be wrong. It felt so right.

Before she could think of all the complications behind that statement, his lips were on hers. Not kissing right away, but imprinting, reminding her what they were. As if she needed reminding. Just as she thought it, her response shocked her again. Heart racing, sensations flying, chest fluttering.

She wanted more. Her mouth opened, and he took the invitation. She couldn't help the moan that escaped. And as if that was what he'd been waiting for, and nothing else, he pulled away.

"Ahem!" She cleared her throat.

"Better get that carpet ready. I think we're gonna have a whole lot to shove under it after tonight." He moved the coffee table and pulled her down in the place where it had been.

She was not going to let herself worry about what that might mean exactly. "Good to know we're both on the same page," she said.

And then there were no more words. Just hands tugging, fingers exploring, hips raising, trembling, trembling. They had never used condoms when they were in high school. She'd been on the pill, and now she'd upgraded to an IUD, but they should have tonight. He was with someone else. And he knew nothing about her history. But he'd tossed the condom from her hand when she'd fumbled in her purse to find it.

"Nothing between us," he said.

Except a wife. Unravelling, unravelling. She was getting the word's significance again. And it was terrifying and incredible all at the same time. The bursting of fifteen years of tension didn't help.

"Yes, yes," she said, as she felt him make contact between her legs. She gasped, raised her hips and arched her back. It was everything. There was no way to convince herself otherwise. "Fuck," she said. And that's what they did.

SEVENTEEN

EMMA

"Hey, you."

Was Michael Kavanagh really in her bed? She couldn't believe it, after all this time. She looked over at him, fast asleep on her pillow. What was he thinking about? After last night, she had every right to think it was probably her. A person couldn't fake that kind of reaction, could they? She was meant to know this by getting everything out in the open, but words hadn't played much of a role last night.

But she knew what she was thinking: all that time she'd kinda sorta thought he was the right one and she'd probably fucked it up, and she'd been right. This was her destiny. And she'd missed out on it. Taylors didn't do coulda woulda shoulda. They fixed or looked forward. And she'd made the decision long ago to look forward. And then with this latest temptation, she was to get in and get out, rather than spend another decade missing him as he went home to his wife. Oh, but what a terrible feeling that left in her chest.

Still, she was probably confusing attraction and love. Yes, it felt perfect now, but there was more to life than feelings. There were wives. And there was the crap Candace was always going on about: *it's not healthy to spend so much time alone*. But even Candace, who knew her Michael issues best, had warned her off married men. But Candace hated her.

"What's going on in that brain? I can see steam coming out," Michael said, his nose inches from hers.

"Oh, you're awake."

"Thought you dreamed me?"

"Screw you," he said, the eyebrow casting its spell.

"Already did that."

He flipped over and pulled her closer.

This was profoundly nice. And hot. Him being friendly this morning wasn't going to change the fact that this was hot—make that ridiculously hot—sex and nothing more. But the puzzle piece rationalization she'd been using last night didn't seem to fit anymore. Mainly because she didn't want him to leave. Ever. What was this alternate universe she'd stepped into and why hadn't she been here all this time? There was no other way to think about it. *Except that he was a married man*. And this was very, very wrong.

No. No. She'd got what she wanted and that was that. Already, she was likely to spend a lifetime feeling guilty for what she'd done to Corner Girl's husband.

Only she then proceeded to get what she wanted. Twice more. Sure, there was guilt. But there was desire, and that seemed to have a momentum of its own.

And then there was talking. But not about the important things. Because why would they do the right thing now?

And there was feeling light and carefree the way she thought only her favorite nightgown (ripped), blanket (smelly), and tea (drugged), could do.

Only better.

And then she got what she wanted again. This time without him getting anything in return. She was going to hell. *So you might as well enjoy it.*

"So, what do we do now?" she asked, pushing her hair back from her face. She had literally worked up a sweat.

"Breakfast?"

And by breakfast he meant take a shower and do it again.

"This is getting out of hand," She said, when they watched the sky deepen to an incredible pink, the sun dipping. "Pizza?"

"You don't still get all those veggies on your pizza, do you?" Michael asked, a towel at his waist.

"You don't still get all that meat on your pizza, do you?"

"Half and half it is, then," Michael said.

God, it was easy to slip back into this.

It should have felt weirder.

Then suddenly, intrusively, halfway through the half and half pizza, it was on the tip of her tongue: what about the wife in the pictures? Her mind traced over the golden hoop earring at the corners of his photos. But she told it to go away. And it did.

"What about you? You sweeping stuff under the carpet, too?" Emma asked, unready, but diving into the weeds all the same. Why did she have to go and ruin everything with the truth? Because he was married. That's why.

"Me? Nah. I like to deal with things."

What about your wife? was at the tip of her tongue.

She just needed to open her mouth and let the words out.

But she didn't.

THEY WALKED along the shore from Kailua Beach Park to Lanikai. This time they'd made it all the way up and down the hill, and were on the way back.

"What if you spend Thanksgiving with me?" Michael said.

"We can't do that. I have to see my parents."

"Your parents? You said you couldn't get a ticket until after Thanksgiving, and that Candace uninvited you."

Shit.

"Come on. I'm sure you miss all my aunties and uncles pressuring you for details about us."

"But I don't have any information."

"Sure, you do. You know what you know." He squeezed her hand in that way. Oh, did she know.

Body reduced to a puddle aside, she should have probed further on that point. But she didn't.

"Well, maybe I will go. But only because all your aunties and uncles have probably missed me so badly."

"Sure, they've missed you. But"—he pulled her onto his lap on the low stone wall, their cheek bones touching—"I've been missing you far more."

She tried to cover how much that affected her by warning every feature of hers not to move even an inch. Pointless, most likely. This was the problem with people who really knew you. She plowed on with the Steely Ms. Taylor anyhow. "Besides, you've got your dad; it's why you're here in the first place."

For a second, she saw the bravado slip from his body. It wasn't nice to witness. Especially since she'd never seen it before.

"He'll be thrilled when he realizes I've been spending time with you." She was too scared to look him in the face to gauge his expression. This was all suddenly very real.

"Okay, I let you get away with a gorgeous comment like that once, but now you've done it twice in as many minutes, so I have to ask: are we pretending we're different people now? The kind who say those types of things—the things they actually mean—to each other?"

"Don't do that. We're older now. And we've screwed this up before. Let's give it a chance. Let's do this." *Wife?*

This was a good man. How could she *not* have faith that he didn't have a good explanation for everything? *Because he hadn't addressed it.*

And the idea of his warm and wonderful family having positive feelings about a bond between them was intensely satisfying. If she mentioned Michael, her dad would probably say, "Who?" And Mom would flick her an article about the dangers of going backward. But they certainly wouldn't have *missed* Michael. She wasn't sure they missed *her* when she wasn't around. Which wasn't the same thing as saying they didn't love her or want her around. Because they did. But they'd be fine without her, too. And she'd had to learn to be fine without them, too. How many eardrum bashing school concerts had her father gotten out of by having to take a last-minute trip to Korea, or to entertain an Indian Four Star General? They knew where they stood and didn't take these things personally.

Which is how she'd treated Michael, even though he wasn't a Taylor. But she *didn't* feel that way about Michael. She *did* need him. And she owed it to herself to explore what that meant. Whether or not it would be the unravelling of her.

"Okay, I'll go."

"Great. Now, I've got another question for you," Michael said, followed by a slight tug on the side of his mouth.

"Yeah?"

"Would you like to take the rest of this week off and go away with me? Again the tug. Was he nervous?

"You mean on a holiday?" Emma bit her lip to keep herself from smiling like an idiot.

"Why not? I'm not ready to go back to reality. You?" His right brow jumped slightly. But she didn't miss it.

She wanted to press more. To ask about his wife. But it

wasn't the right time. And she was beginning to realize it was turning out never to be the right time.

But whatever was going on there, clearly it must not be good. He'd been here for a couple of weeks now, and his wife wasn't spending Thanksgiving with him. He needed this. *They* needed this. And if they extended whatever this was to a holiday, then they could milk it for all it was worth before it all went to pieces, which it most likely would.

Because despite the words he'd said earlier, she didn't trust this. It was certainly no fairy tale. This was the 21st century, where men sent women pictures of their dicks and lost congressional seats, possibly because the world was addicted to CBD, a world where sex had knocked love out of first place, and it had all become mechanical and ugly.

But not the way they did it. "Where should we go?" She grinned despite the idiocy factor.

Which was just fine, because he did, too.

EIGHTEEN

EMMA

Three hours later they approached the rundown Honolulu Airport in yet another Uber. Instead of trying to navigate the perplexingly-signed complex, they could lean into the backseat and leave it to the Uber driver to find the inter-island departure terminal.

When they arrived, they looked for signs for Hawaiian Airlines, the only carrier currently offering inter-island flights, and, of course, couldn't find one. They both turned in opposite directions and started walking. It only took a few seconds until Michael called her over to a small placard cunningly hidden by a palm leaf.

"I was right," he said.

"I know you think you're a master navigator, but it just so happens that that location is a temporary arrangement. Don't get too cocky. Hawaiian Airlines is usually over there." Emma thumbed behind her.

"Interesting how we both went in opposite directions."

"I don't see it as very interesting." She squinted. "This airport is a clusterfuck. Everyone knows that."

"But I went one way, and you immediately chose the other. Don't you find that interesting?" This time his inner brow lowered. Was he going to get serious on her?

"No. Why should I trust *you* over my own instincts?" It was clear this wasn't about the terminal navigation any longer. Emma forced herself to shut her mouth and led them in Michael's direction. If they hadn't talked about anything serious up until now, why would they choose the start of a paradisiacal, spur-of-the-moment getaway to ruin the moment?

"You should trust me."

"We'll see."

In flight, Michael had nearly made her spill her complimentary guava juice. She'd closed her eyes for a second, and he put his hand over hers. She'd wished she was ready to open her eyes and show him how it had affected her, but she didn't dare. Sex was one thing. Meaningful caresses were something quite different.

After that, their knees were touching the whole time, like they couldn't help themselves. And she convinced herself this was easier to deal with. Sex was sex. It didn't have to lead to unravelling. She was headed to paradise with Michael Kavanagh. Why not roll with the fantasy? If her reasoning wasn't sitting quite as squarely as it had before, she wasn't ready to admit it.

THEY PICKED UP A RED MUSTANG, which was the most popular vehicle to rent in Hawaii, and rode with the top down to the Hilton resort. The traffic wasn't surprising. But it was getting hot in the sun, and so it was a relief when they arrived at the hotel grounds, manicured to within an inch of its life. She told herself it was the perfect environment for something as artificial as they were creating between them—an escape from reality, was the way she'd tried to frame it in the car ride. And in doing so, she'd allowed herself to relax a bit. They could be whatever they wished with each other on the Big Island. Reality could whack them later.

In the elevator, the bellman was at the helm of an extraordinarily large gold cart carrying only their two small overnight bags, and there was Michael's hand again, this time on the small of her back. He let his finger play at the hem of her top and then beneath. He moved south and tucked his finger inside the waist of her skirt. It only took him a second to realize she didn't have underwear on. Why should she on Fantasy Island? His head jerked and she pretended not to notice. Let him think this modern-day Emma went commando all the time. Turned out, she was excellent at fantasy. She should have tried it long ago.

They followed the bellman to the room while Emma pretended she had no idea Michael would be watching her walk. They were shown how to use the coffee machine, push aside the curtains, and anything else that might garner him a tip, which Michael overgenerously supplied, as half his family worked in the tourist trade. The sound of the bellman's cart safely fading down the endless corridor, Michael pulled her up against the door and they repeated their performance from earlier. Only vertically. Surely this would get old soon?

"Feel that?" he asked, after.

"What?"

"You know," he said, and placed a finger on her lips so she wouldn't dissent.

All part of the fantasy, she told herself. If she wanted to believe it was love he was referring to, she would allow it. But only on Fantasy Island.

This time when they showered together, Michael was territorial. Soaped up her back, kissed her, kneeled, put his mouth on her thigh, licked so close, until she was pushing him into her. It was never like this. They had been too young back then. But his wife might have enjoyed this treatment. No, she wasn't going there now.

Afterward, they opened a bottle of red on the lanai. They'd paid a fortune for it in the resort's convenience shop, but it was rich, velvety, and she closed her eyes to savor the moment. The ridiculously perfect moment. Was any of this really happening?

"Come here, you." He placed her drink on the table between their chairs and pulled her onto his lap and kissed her neck. They looked up at the cluster of stars over the ocean, which was hushing its soft waves hypnotically along the shore.

They ate dinner at the resort's seafood restaurant. It was decadent and overpriced and not nearly as good as anything she would have eaten at her mother's house. But they savored the attention, the detail, the pink hibiscus on the plate, the pearls of butter in their minimalist square dish. During the meal, they tried very hard not to laugh at some Europeans at a neighboring table who asked, "What is this *spom*?"

Full, they took their mai tais to the beach. On the sand, he pulled her to sit between his legs, and they stared up at the enormous sky. "Would you like to see my *spom*?" he asked.

She swatted him. "How long have you been waiting to say that?"

It was too good, so she forced herself to think of all of Candace's real-life stories: congealed pasta on the floor, explosive poo-poo nappies, not wanting to be touched by Tom or anyone else for weeks on end. But even that wouldn't stick. And why should it? This was fantasy time. She was allowed. She would let herself indulge. Besides, it was unlikely Candace would be around to smash her 'gushing with poo-poo nappies' ever again.

The night was incredible. They talked more than she'd talked with anyone, and more honestly, too, than she had in years. They laughed and argued about old times. Even the meaningful caresses became more natural. Emma found herself reaching for Michael more often. It was impossible to reconcile the days she'd spent fantasizing about a mere digital exchange with Michael with the experience of being here with him. Had it really been so difficult to accept his friend request and so simple to get back into bed with him?

TOO QUICKLY, the first night rolled into the second, and the third. It was five o'clock after a long day of sex, indulgent food, and incredible surfing.

"I'm gonna hit the shower," Michael said, his arms stretching overhead and then pulling her close, onto his chest.

"And then what? The pool?"

"Definitely."

It was their third night. They'd gotten into the habit of watching the sunset with mai tais accompanied by the sounds of the Jack Johnson-esque guitarist at the pool bar. It was all part of the manufactured image of *Hawaii Nei*, she knew that. But it grew easier to ignore that after a couple of days of luxury.

"I'll head in after you," she said, and laid back on the bed to close her eyes for a second. Then she grew fidgety and picked up her phone, though she hated the idea of using it to pass the time. Surely, there were better things to do in Paradise? But she wanted to check in for any emails from Candace, despite her living in the fantasy mantras. There weren't any.

And then a Facebook alert pinged up on his phone, with the message bubble: Watch out, Oahu, Patricia's coming to town!

Patricia? Did she know a Patricia? Despite the voice that told her it was probably a virus just waiting to unleash untold damage to her phone, she clicked on the alert. And there, in the profile picture alongside the post, she saw the one thing that could bring her tumbling out of Paradise faster than a serpent with an apple. The earrings! It was her, Corner Girl, Michael's wife. Emma's chest went cold. Right before her eyes, another post popped up from Patricia.

Michael's little lady is coming to town to keep an eye on him. We all know he gets into mischief when he's let loose. Clear your calendars everyone!

She threw the phone and it landed with a thunk on the floral carpet. Emma had convinced herself that Michael and his wife were over. But this told a whole different story. What *was* going on with him? Was she in Paradise with a bad guy, who was screwing over his innocent wife, just to show himself there was still someone who thought he was special?

The bathroom door opened.

"What was that?" Michael asked.

"The future."

"What?"

"Never mind," she said. Her mind reeled, but the one thing she wasn't going to do was speak rashly. She had to think.

At sunset drinks Michael asked if there was anything wrong. "You're awfully quiet."

"Am I? How long do you have off?" she asked.

"I thought we were meant to be avoiding reality?"

"It had to end sometime." All that time thinking of what to say and that's what she'd come out with? Amazing.

"Okay, I don't know, what about you?" There was that tug at the side of his mouth again.

There could be lots of reasons he would look nervous, but why did her suspicions keep landing on dishonesty? "I've got to be in the office on Thursday." She tried to ignore the *deja vu* the silence between them brought on. This was how it had been in Paris.

To his credit, Michael didn't push the issue. And to hers, she hadn't taken it further. Which was good because she had no idea how to address the question. If it was time for honesty, she needed to be honest with herself. And that meant this time with Michael had changed her, had affected her more than she would like to admit. And she needed to get this right.

To that end, that night Emma had pretended to be asleep when he got out of the shower. It killed her, but she didn't move a muscle, though his arms were around her and his breath was on her neck. All she could think of was *Patricia*. All she could think to say about her was confrontational. Was *he* worrying this much over the matter?

The next day, they drove around the island to Volcanoes National Park. After the tourist resort areas, there were miles of nothing. Her mind seemed to have a blockade up on the Patricia front. The more she focused on the problem, the less clarity was shed on it.

As she watched the scenery blaze by, Emma let her mind wander. Most people would find it hard to live like this, with no choice of supermarkets, one or two dining options, and no shopping to speak of. But she could easily picture herself here, raising chickens, growing fruits and veggies. In fact, she thought of her client, how they would attract the local demographic if they could extend their face-to-face plan to a place like this.

Why not have pop-up shops at remote spots in vacation destinations, rather than in the manufactured environment of the resorts? Traffic was the only barrier. But they could bring the people out here; it would get people out into the real life of the places they visited. It was a great idea. And would benefit the communities, too. Millions of people funneled through here to get from resorts to Kilauea. There was barely anything to stop at in-between.

She could sort out all the problems of the world but couldn't get to square one with her own problems. *Patricia.* She had to say something. It would kill her otherwise.

"What's wrong?" Michael asked after a too-quiet stretch of highway.

Would he have seen Patricia's post? Would he be looking forward to seeing her? What would happen now? She could feel herself scanning for an escape route. And that was probably the right thing to do.

Soon enough, the volcano emerged in the distance. She was taken aback by the smoldering power of it. There was a plume of smoke snaking from the peak. Was that molten lava she saw? The glowing redness of it alarmed her. It was beautiful, yes. But dangerous, too. It made sure you didn't walk away without being clear on that.

"I don't like it." She hadn't known she was going to say that.

"Why not?"

"It's terrifying."

"What's terrifying about it?" Michael said.

"Why don't you ask all those people in Pompeii?"

"Sure, but these are modern times. We evacuate when activity picks up."

"Doesn't mean we're prepared, or that everyone will be saved."

He didn't answer.

At the entrance to the park, tour buses were parked as far as the eye could see.

HUNDREDS OF TOURISTS waited in a line for who knew what: tickets? Maps? But they followed blindly, unthinkingly, like the kind of people she always hated. At an unmarked counter, Emma grabbed a map and fingered the location they should drive to first. As they walked back to the car, she wondered what they were doing here. The tone of the trip had shifted. Michael's phone jingled and she could feel the hairs on the back of her neck stand on end.

Couldn't the man turn his ringer off? Wouldn't that be the first thing you'd do if you were trying to bury your head in the sand? He pulled it out of his pocket, and she had a clear view and saw it was Patricia. A text message. *On my way!* There was no avoiding it any longer. He saw her see. She kept walking but he pulled her back.

"Stop," he said.

"Why?"

"We need to talk about her."

"About who?"

"I know you saw the post from Patricia. I don't think it was any coincidence that the post notification came up when I was in the shower and then I found my phone in the far corner of the room behind the rubbish bin."

"That could be a coincidence."

Michael cocked his head. He didn't look guilty enough. Shouldn't he be feeling remorseful?

"Yes. You got a notification on your phone when you were in the shower. It popped up right there on the screen and there was no avoiding it. I didn't go snooping. Believe me, I didn't want to see that."

He let out a huge sigh, looked around, as if for a way to protect himself when this all went bad. "That's why I hate technology," he said. "Nothing looks the way it really is."

"That sounds like something a cheater might say," she said. A large group moving past them seemed to swallow them up.

"Is that what you think of me?" he whispered as the tourists in matching red shirts filed along.

"Yup. Your little lady is coming. That's what it said. Oh, you know what? Maybe we'll run into her at the airport! Wouldn't that be cozy?" Emma noticed her voice get louder. A couple of people turned to look as her face burned.

"Calm down," Michael said.

"You want me to calm down."

"Well, you can get all worked up about it if you want to."

"Get worked up about what, exactly?"

"That's my point. You don't even know."

"Look, we can do the whole Romeo and Juliet, where we're talking over each other, not paying attention, and it's a horrible mistake that ends tragically, nobody really knowing the truth, or we can put it all on the table right now. I know this is just a fantasy. I told you that a hundred times. You're going to go back to your life and I'm going back to mine. Does this really change anything? The truth is—"

"You're gonna tell me what the truth is?"

"Why don't you just let me guess, see how good my instinct is?"

"That's the complete opposite of what you just said you wanted to do, but go ahead."

She was vaguely aware that she was acting desperately, all in hopes of shutting down the uncomfortable situation. And it seemed more than likely this was similar to how things had played out back in Paris. Why was she so protective? After all that extending the benefit of the doubt, here she was smashing all the trust to bits.

"You're married," she said. "Having a bit of a rough patch. Decided to come and find someone who you knew would be here pining over you, make you feel special again."

"Ugly way to put it, but—"

"But true?"

"You're missing some facts."

"Oh, am I? You know what? Never mind. I thought I could be modern. I thought I could be happy mastering twenty ways to orgasm before sunset, but it turns out I'm not. There. You were wrong all along. I fucking needed you. I needed you then and I need you now. At least there's one truth we got out in the end here. And while we're at it, *that's* why I let you walk away in Paris, pushed you out the door the second you hinted at leaving. Because it fucking terrified me how insecure I felt over there by myself, without you. That wasn't me. Or at least I didn't want it to be. I could go anywhere, do anything before you came along. Then suddenly, I couldn't. Well, I got over that. All I had to do was remove the risk. That's what Taylors do. We're strong. We don't make a big deal about it. If going straight ahead isn't an option, you go around. You get what you get, and you don't get upset. And the difference now is, it's going to be easy to get over you. Because you're a lying asshole." *Way to not go talking over him! Congrats for the slow and steady approach.*

There were Japanese tourists taking photos of them. One stepped in front and used a selfie stick for the shot. She decided to let it go. If the tables were turned, she'd probably be making faces behind the scene-makers' backs.

"Glad we didn't do the talking over each other thing."

"Thank god I had you to point that out to me! I'm going to go back to the room to pack my bags and go home." *Don't. Let him speak. What are you so afraid of?*

He grabbed for her wrist. "Don't. I didn't tell the whole truth, but—" His lids were lowered. He looked so sad.

She wanted more than anything to hear him out. Have him say something to make it all right. But he didn't finish the sentence, and in the silence, she grew terrified of how he might. "No. Never mind. Don't try and be a hero. Don't try to fix it.

Because I don't want you to. This is the way I want it. After all these years, I finally believe it. I don't fucking need anyone. What a relief. I should thank you." *Liar.*

"You're welcome."

She started to walk away, but then remembered he had to drive her all the way back to Kona.

"Can we talk?" he asked as he dropped the key in his lap in front of the steering wheel.

"What shall we talk about? Cheating? Inflated egos that allow men to justify fucking around on their wives? Women who are stupid enough to go along with it?"

He opened his mouth to respond and Emma cut him off. What was she doing? Why wouldn't she let the man speak? She could feel herself trying her best to repel him. "You know what?" She put her palm in his face, in a way she would have batted away, but which he allowed with no more than a slight tightening of his eyelids. "I'm sick of those topics. Haven't thought about much else since you messaged your way back into my life!"

"I knew you were good at avoiding thoughts that make you uncomfortable, but this is beyond the pale, even for you, Emma." He gripped the key tightly, she could see his arm muscles tense.

He was looking so intensely at her she had to turn away. There was smoke in the distance, at the volcano's summit.

"You want to talk about beyond the pale? How about lying? How about cheating? Please. Whatever this was, it's done. Do not speak to me."

He closed his eyes and drew a long breath. She could see him rearranging the muscles in his jaw. She admired his ability to stay quiet.

Already she was in regret mode and they hadn't even left the lot.

It was a long ride.

Finally, she could see their hotel's highest tower in the distance.

"Can we talk?" he asked, as he turned off the ignition at the car park.

Her hand was already on the door. "No. You give me ten minutes to clear my stuff out of the room, and let's leave it at that."

"You don't mean it. Can't you give me a chance to explain?"

"Okay, tell me you're not married to a woman who likes to wear tiny golden hoop earrings!"

"I cannot deny that."

"Well, then, that's that. You'd better leave me to it before I start responding to Patricia's posts on Facebook."

He shut his eyes and shook his head. But he let her go. Again.

Emma wished he hadn't. She wished he'd told her Patricia and he were divorced, that she was stalking him and there was a rationalization for everything. She hadn't given him a chance. And while that seemed a valuable offense, now it looked juvenile, and selfish. For someone who'd been so hell-bent on trusting him, she'd certainly declared his verdict before the trial. She should walk back to that car, from where she could feel his eyes on her back.

But she didn't.

NINETEEN

MICHAEL

My wife wanted kids. That was the beginning of the end for us. I knew, in all good conscience, I could not bring a child into this world with a woman I did not love. It wasn't right, my having gotten us into this mess, and I felt terrible about it. There was no excuse.

The first time we'd come home from visiting a couple of new parents from our friend group in Boston, Patricia didn't speak the whole way home. I knew it the second she held that baby. I was scum. I was worse than scum. We rode the T and it was freaking freezing, and I wasn't about to start this conversation in public. The train stood still for a good twenty minutes during which she did not look at me once. I saw her wiping tears from her eyes, and I felt like the worst kind of asshole. What kind of man marries a woman he isn't properly in love with? How could I have let it get so far? Because love is a clusterfuck, I tell myself in my more generous moments. But there were no excuses for my behavior. It was my fault and mine alone. I should have known better.

When Maku (which Mom insisted I call her if she was going to have a *haole* name like Kavanagh; she was joking, but not really) was sick, I'd flown home from Boston and stayed for about three months. I'd only been seeing Patricia for three months previous to that, and things began to move unnaturally fast. Especially since I knew Mother wanted more than anything to see me happy, and ready to grow the family. Pure Hawaiians were a significant minority and her family never missed a chance to make a crack at Maku about her *haole* son which was technically incorrect; I was *hapa*, or "half." They didn't really mean it; they loved me and knew Maku was happy and that was all that mattered to them, but they never liked to pass up an opportunity for a "loving" jab; this was our idea of humor. I could beat every one of them out in the surf by the time I was fourteen, so I simply used that as my "loving" jab. Dad mostly kept quiet and drank beer. He was not an alcoholic, he explained, he was Irish. And besides, Maku only let him have one a night, so he drank it very slowly.

One night, when Maku took a turn for the worse, I spent the better part of the evening into dawn talking to Patricia on the telephone about all the memories I had. I knew it was not the way men were meant to act, and I certainly wouldn't have said any of it to Dad, but Patricia had a way of coaxing things out of me; she was incredibly non-judgmental. By the time the sun came up, I had asked her to marry me, promising to bring a huge rock back to Boston. I was making good money and I could afford it. I tried not to think about the images from the past that were sending up questions in the periphery of my mind. The past was the past. Everyone knew that. And they also knew that we rewrote memories to suit whatever we needed to feel like crap about at present.

Besides, once I'd made the decision, it took on a momentum of its own. As if it wasn't me proposing, but a massive thing happening all of its own that I just happened to be around to witness. I could almost convince myself it was the right thing because it made Maku and everyone else so happy when nothing else had for so long. The rest was history. And brought us to that terrible moment on the T, after which hours of crying and yelling ensued.

At one of the lowest points of the arguing after the T ride of silence, Patricia yelled out, "I know what this is really about. I know that you aren't over her! That Emma from high school. You say her name most nights when you sleep. And I shouldn't have been surprised with how absent and cold you are with me!"

It was terrible to hear how badly I'd hurt her, how much attention she'd put toward trying to work out my motivations and desires on her own. She thought that over time I'd forget about what she called my "high school sweetheart" and that we would be passionate the way she believed we once were.

But she was wrong about something: what we had wasn't love. It was only ever attraction, and then comfort that felt great, but it was never love.

That night after the train we had both agreed, at least I thought we had, that having kids was never going to happen. That it was a terrible tragedy and that I was completely in the wrong, but we should end it now before kids were in the picture.

When I went to bed that night on a friend's couch, I thought the worst of it was behind us. But I had no idea.

TWENTY

EMMA

Emma ran back to the hotel room and gathered her belongings, trying to ignore the maid arranging chocolates on her pillow. Her clothing had been neatly folded and stacked on the dresser, so it only took a few moments to stuff it in her bag.

Toiletries had also been stylishly grouped, and so she swept those into her dob kit in a matter of seconds. In her current mood, there was a distinct satisfaction in wrecking the orderly display. Everything shouldn't look so perfect when her life was anything but. In fact, the whole room looked off-putting to her now; it was everything that was wrong with not only Hawaii, but the world in general. She checked all the essentials: wallet, phone, keys. All set. Good riddance. *Mahalo* for nothing.

This airport was lots more outdated and shabbier than Oahu's, and she couldn't even find the origin of the line she needed to join in the cluster of all the other lines. The result was that she was booked out of the next two flights and had to wait three hours, which she spent picking at a depressed, wilted salad with a dressing whose fat content she wasn't going to begin to think about. She should have ordered the pizza. *Always go with the pizza when the selection sucks.*

By all rights, she should have been somewhere that the pizza doesn't suck: Italy. She should have planned early and been there now. There were a heck of a lot of "should haves" in her life at the moment, and she was going to have to start to face them.

On cue she looked up and saw Michael five tables away, about to bite into a puffy-crusted meat pizza.

She picked up her food and walked calmly and unpanicked to the farthest part of the tiny airport. Which was not very far. She faced the other direction and found herself next to a newlywed couple who couldn't keep their hands off each other. *I should tell them*, she thought. *I should tell them what really happened in marriages: the husband takes his ring off and screws the one who got away at the first opportunity.*

Who was she kidding? They wouldn't listen to her.

This world was worse than she thought. It was good that she'd be alone in it. She could fill her house with luxurious blankets so that when one got stinky, she'd just grab another, and go around feeling them, like a toddler. That's where she'd been headed before Michael had come back into her life, and it had been just fine with her.

She told herself she would not turn around and look at him. And she didn't. Except three times, during which she pretended to try to get a better signal on her phone. The phone was off, but the kissing fish alongside her wouldn't know. And if they did say anything, then she *would* tell them about their future.

On the third time, she saw Michael catch her eye. He smiled. He really thought this was going to be okay. She wouldn't give him the benefit of a reaction. Look how that had turned out in the car. She'd gone from patient and trusting to hysterical in no time. Instead, Emma turned back around and got a neck ache trying to keep her shoulders straight. That would show him.

The plane was small, and she prayed they would be seated far away from each other. When they called her section, she made sure she was first in line and refused to look where Michael had been standing at the far end of the seating area.

There was a tap on her shoulder, and she refused to turn around. "Don't speak to me."

"Ummmm, ma'am, you dropped your boarding pass."

She about-faced, grumbled an apology to an older gentleman in large eyeglasses and a drugstore Hawaiian shirt, and bent down to pick up the pass. When she stood back up, there Michael was, about six people back. Again, he smiled. What was with that? She was gonna wipe that thing right off his face. He was still on trial for cheating here, despite her rampage, no?

In the achingly long wait to get into her seat, during which people took an inexplicable amount of time to arrange their shopping bags of macadamia nuts and lilikoi syrup in the overhead compartments, she gave in twice, and swiveled to look at him, pretending not to. Both times he was grinning, like the cat who ate the canary. What the hell? She tried not to think about him, but of course that made it impossible to think of anything else. Was that what he was laughing about?

Though he was seated five rows ahead of her, throughout the flight he did not turn around. No more grins for her. Good. But why didn't he? Why had he suddenly stopped doing his psychotic smiling thing?

For the rest of the flight she fought back tears. She was a terrible person who wanted him despite Patricia, his wife. That was really why she'd been so angry—and not only at him. Now that she'd allowed herself to find out that she wanted him for deadly certain, she couldn't have him. It all grew more complicated from there, because despite how deeply she desired him—not just physically but in every way she could ever dream of connecting with another person—the evidence showed he was a lying, cheating bastard and that she'd known this and gone ahead with the whole thing anyway. He'd simply been using her to boost his ego, while at home, he was probably prosaically leaving dirty socks on the floor and hassling Patricia for caring about the dishes instead of wanting to have sex. But what would she go home to? Blankets. Fucking blankets. And she couldn't even convince herself she wanted them anymore. It wasn't even cold in Hawaii. What good was a blanket, for crying out loud?

And the worst part was that this was Emma's own fault. She knew about the status and she'd chosen not to confront him about it. And even before that, she'd suspected. Was what she'd referred to as trust in Michael actually just self-deception?

She stared ahead of her during the whole flight, rejecting the pineapple shortbread and the POM juice, which now looked like a beverage choice for a person who wanted all the world's sweetness and couldn't choose, so just took everything.

There was a moment on the open tarmac, as she made her way to the terminal, when she saw his shadow approaching her. She felt a weak-kneed terror. But when his hand reached for her shoulder, she felt something even worse. The fucking tears started to spill. She picked up her rolling case and ran.

Despite his quiet sensibility, she heard him scream her name, once, twice, three times. "Please!" he yelled.

But she didn't look back. Inside the Charlie's taxi, she tried again to get out the words of her address through choking sobs. The guy must have understood the town name, at least, because he headed in the right direction. But when he pulled up to a building, it wasn't Emma's. She didn't even know where she was.

She got out though, gave him a huge tip, as if that might

make up for all the bad judgements she'd made in the past, and found her way to Kailua Beach Park to watch the sunset. She tried to think of it as symbolic, beautiful, the end of something, which would mean the start of something else. But it just seemed to happen too quickly, lots of beautiful pinks and yellows stringing through the sky, looking like a miracle. Then suddenly nothing.

TWENTY-ONE

EMMA

This is where someone would get upset, drink lots of wine, and sit home listening to sad music. But that spill in the taxi had been enough to snap her into action. She wasn't going to sit around and mope. She was going to work her ass off on that account she'd just landed her company and put her money where her mouth was. She would not waste one second thinking about Michael. *Patricia!* Probably she should unfriend him. But not yet. That seemed too childish. And she'd done enough childish things to even the score between them, if she was going to let herself think about that. Which she was not.

Friday morning, she was still at the office after having pulled a Thanksgiving all-nighter. She almost convinced herself it felt good to be the only one there. She'd accomplished a ton. In fact, she'd engaged a couple of incredible illustrators to try to capture the visuals of the campaign. She was very much looking forward to what they came up with.

As she poured herself a large water from the cooler, she

listened to the sound of her long-term marketing plan for D.N.E. judder through the printer.

She thought of Candace, with her lovely family, pretending she wasn't upset about the loss of her best friend. Maybe she wasn't. Maybe Candace was relieved to be rid of her and focus on family.

That didn't sit right, though. Too simplistic. But Emma was so unhappy she forced the narrative into place. She felt the tears already, that terrible pricking at her eyes, the swirl of her vision. She was getting used to them, unpalatable as that might be for her.

Later that day, she'd be on a flight to Italy. She had calls out to dozens of vendors and the logistics would be sorted out after the holiday. Probably by Candace. Who would also probably never speak to her again.

Emma needed to reach out. She'd hurt her friend. She knew that; she'd also known that something strange was going on with Candace, but hadn't bothered to find out what. So, the CBD incident wasn't entirely to blame for their friendship meltdown.

What I did at that meeting—as your friend—was completely out of line. More than anything, I want to apologize for that.

By the time she'd cleared customs, this time with five minutes to run to her gate, she still hadn't received any kind of response from Candace. Why should she?

Emma sank into her seat and prepared for the long haul. No sooner had she stowed her bag overhead than an announcement buzzed over the P.A. that there would be an hour delay on her take-off. It turned out to be more like forty-five minutes, but after that, it was all smooth sailing. She had a row of empty seats for lying down—an unforeseen benefit of missing Thanksgiving, free booze, a good movie, and even a Michael-free nap.

But when she woke, she was furious all over again, freshly so, as if her furiousness had spawned new offshoots to become something unrecognizable and monstrous. Sure, she hadn't handled things well, but how could Michael put her in this situation? How could she allow it to happen? It was so obviously a terrible idea from the outset. She should have seen this coming. How else would it end up but in disaster?

The most surprising part of the journey was just how much she'd needed the hug her mother gave her at the gate. She wasn't going to allow herself a repeat of what she had come to think of, over the course of free booze and mind-grinding, as *the ugly thing*, which most people benignly called crying. Instead, she closed her eyes and appreciated every ounce of pressure her mother applied to her back.

"How's our little soldier." It wasn't a question. Emma was fine. Taylors were fine.

"Great, Mom."

"Don't worry. We'll fatten you up. Lots of pasta going on here."

Emma caught herself pathetically scanning the door her fellow international passengers had emerged from customs through. She hadn't expected Michael to pull a white knight and find his way onto her flight to make things right again. And yet...

"Dad's home making pasta from scratch. It's his new favorite thing; even put a pizza oven in." Why would two people come to pick her up when only one was necessary? That practical thinking had never bothered her before, and she wasn't going to let it now. Perhaps *never* wasn't exactly correct, but normally she wouldn't think twice, could shake the slight irritation at his not coming to the airport like any other normal fucking parent. But it had been a long time since she'd seen her father. And Emma was starting to realize she was in a fragile state—whether or not the idea of such a thing was abhorrent to her.

Her parents' house, or villa, rather, was amazing. Stone walls, perfectly rustic finishes, brocade couch, carved woodwork, and huge oil paintings covering nearly every inch of wall in the dim space. It was at once ancient and original with all the mod cons, and it struck her that this was precisely the kind of balance she'd been after for her client. Maybe it was in her blood.

Slowly, the stress rolled from her shoulders as she watched her newly svelte Dad roll out the dough. They drank an incredible Barolo waiting for the dough to rise. Her mother was already upstairs somewhere, as if she could see Emma any old time. But in this environment, and under the calming effect of the heavy red, she considered that maybe her mother *could* manage such a feat; it was as if time worked differently here. Like she could feel every second of the day and that each one begged to be filled with simple pleasures. Yes, she was returning to herself. Maybe she could even find a new blanket while she was here—an Italian one. One that would take the place of this needy hunger for a human touch.

This was just where she needed to be. After the first night's sleep in her chilly tower room, cozied under proper down blankets in ancient covers, she felt rejuvenated, like maybe, in time, she could get past this latest entanglement with Michael and regain some semblance of normalcy. Maybe she would follow what she imagined would be Candace's advice, if Candace didn't hate her, and go "fuck some hot Italian guy." Her body didn't respond to the idea, but there was time. Here, there was plenty of time.

Besides, Michael hadn't reached out to her. Clearly, he was looking to move on, too. With his wife. Care of Emma's verbal steamroll he'd saved himself an ugly conversation, and maybe he'd realized that later on. At least that would explain why he was grinning like the cat that ate the canary every time she'd forsaken her own cardinal rule and turned around to catch his eye.

ON THE SECOND NIGHT, the neighbors came for dinner. It was pizza, and she and her mom spent hours picking, cleaning, and prepping magazine-worthy vegetables for an accompanying salad so beautiful it deserved a new name. Over the chopping board, she told her mom about the new work she'd been doing with D.N.E.

"Great. I was wondering when you'd get your footing there. I knew if you really didn't like it, you'd go."

Her parents always assumed Emma would land on her feet. That she'd instinctively know what to do in any given situation without explanation. She'd been born a small adult in their eyes. If she didn't know the right thing to do, she'd fake it. There was the infamous night she'd been caught necking some gin from a tumbler in her footie pajamas. She didn't even spit it out; she forced herself to drink it down. It's what they did. Obviously, she was meant to know how it was done. Emma had grown up assuming this was how everyone was treated.

The first guests arrived at eight o'clock because, apparently, people ate late in Italy. That was especially nice because it had allowed her time to nap in the afternoon and still have time to check out the cliff walk, which also happened to have the one spot for clear cell phone reception, before she had to dress for the guests. Even the autumn temperature was invigorating. She hadn't been cold for so long. Emma had enjoyed digging through her old boots, scarves and sweaters, even if some of them had become moth-eaten. It was heart-warming that they'd saved them and hauled them all this way, and on the other hand, another way to underline how different everything was here.

Spending time with her parents always ignited a hunger for

change. Like they carried the contagious virus and she caught it. It was one of the reasons she'd kept her distance since settling on Oahu. But now, she felt there was a whole world of other stuff out there she was missing out on. Perhaps this was the next platform for her marketing efforts—the global feel, a reminder that it's a small world. There was something there, and she was sure it would germinate during her stay. That's the way the world worked with them, constantly moving and evolving, even if they didn't know a thing about the turmoil in her life. She told herself it was a relief not to have to discuss it.

The neighbors from the other side arrived next with their two girls—one was three years old and the other was five. The tallest one in shiny black hair was wearing a garish nylon Disney princess gown, tiered with netted "chiffon" to the ground. The younger one was in what must have been an ancient dress-up gown, a dreamy, silky thing with hand-done lace and gems sewn onto the neckline, which made her look like a queen, golden ringlets and all. She carried herself in keeping with the part.

When they spoke Italian, it was gorgeous.

Emma knew Italian; she'd been speaking it since junior high school, along with Japanese, of course, a more useful language, but she'd made sure not to let the Italian dry up. She listened to Italian audiobooks, news podcasts, and, of course, she'd visited her parents here. Being with the locals, she found it rolled off her tongue. *Boh*, she was especially fond of. The only language that could make 'I don't know' sound cool. *Daje* she was also fond of—an encouraging term that sounded incredibly warm rolling off her father's tongue. She probably read too much into it, which was easy to do with Italian, a language that felt nuanced and beautiful.

She busied herself mixing the girls some cordial, making them bread and cheese plates. In turn, they showed her their dolls, which she enjoyed immensely—lovely old things with porcelain heads and appendages with tiny nicks here and there that evidenced the affection they'd been lavished with.

Emma hadn't turned around when the last group arrived. So, she was taken by surprise to see a handsome, light-haired man. He appeared a couple of years her senior and accepted a beer before taking a seat opposite her. "*Ciao,*" he mouthed, dipping his chin.

He wasn't one of those skinny-jeans wearing metrosexuals either. He looked rugged and crisp at the same time. The macho thing could apparently have an effect on her outside of the sphere of Michael. Had her mother set this up on purpose? She doubted her mom would have been obvious about it if she had. It wasn't worth asking, as her mother would not admit to such a thing. And it didn't matter. She told herself she was lucky. She could follow Candace's imaginary advice without having to leave the block. Sure, she wasn't feeling anything resembling excitement at present, but that didn't mean anything, did it? And where had listening to her instincts brought her thus far?

Over drinks, it became clear that Gianni, her new Italian prospect, was renovating a tiny inn at the rear of his family's property. Though he wasn't the one to bring it up, nor to provide most of the details, it was clear from his smile that he was proud of it. He'd worked on her parents' house, too, and so she could only imagine how incredible his own place would be. She caught him zoning out once during the conversation, which was mainly about him, and when he met her eye, he smirked, like somehow they were in the same boat here. She wasn't sure what boat that was. Was it a boat headed for the imaginary Candace's advised destination? She was definitely feeling like she could wind up there if she wanted to.

And of course she wanted to. He was Italian. And sexy as hell. There would be something incredibly wrong with her if she didn't want him. She assured herself she did.

Of course, she didn't know if he had any interest aside from the fact that he'd smirked, but she wasn't going to think about the details too much. Besides, it seemed a lot less far-fetched after a few more Barolos. In fact, she was getting incredibly heavy-limbed and sleepy.

As the table went on and on—in an eighty-ten mixture of Italian and English—about Gianni's labor of love, she couldn't help but think about her job back home. Sure, she'd made some strides, but was she ultimately trying to fit a square peg into a round hole? Was a total independence from all that social media a better fit for her? Was this whole Michael fiasco the universe's way of telling her this?

"You simply must go and see it, Emma," her mother said.

"Yes," Gianni spoke up, turning everyone's head. "You must. *Domani*?" Why did the Italian word for tomorrow have so much more promise in it? Domain, somewhere ahead, to go, to conquer, she thought, stringing associations together. *Domani* she might get to wash that man right out of her hair.

"It would be an honor," she said, trying not to blush at the wishful romantic commentary of the shameless matchmakers her mother had invited into her home. Her mother seemed wildly amused by the whole thing. Perhaps she'd changed, too. Other people's business had never been very much up her alley.

Emma helped her parents to bring out countless dishes in colorful, ancient crockery. Her parents' world here was elegant and full, indulgent and oozing with pleasure. Was she crazy for not just giving in and joining them? What was she doing living somewhere that had only been meant to be a stop along the way, filling her head with pointless could-have-been scenarios about a life that never was?

By the end of the evening she felt full, and even loved; maybe she'd been too hard in her estimation of her parents. But there was that dull thud in her chest reminding her that all was not right. *Everything would be perfect, if only . . .*

But it isn't, she told herself. *It just isn't.*

She helped her mother with the dishes in the kitchen.

"So?" Mother raised her eyebrows. "Gianni?"

"Mother! Are you trying to play matchmaker?" Emma scrubbed hard at a spot in the saucepan.

"What? If I were your age, I'd tap that ass." Her mother shrugged and sipped from a wineglass that may not have been hers.

"Mother!"

"Isn't that how people talk today?"

"Yes, it is. And I think it's gross." She nearly had the burnt bit completely gone. Her hand was getting a workout with the scouring pad.

"You've always been an old soul, Emma." She held the empty wineglass up to inspect it with a questioning expression.

"I'm cutting you off."

"Don't. I'm having so much fun. You must miss living in Europe. When I think back to living in Hawaii, I think of moldy, old produce, traffic jams, shabby tourist traps, and, for the privilege, paying five times as much for it all as we do here. I worry about you there. All alone."

"I'm not alone. You've had too much to drink. Let's not do this now." She didn't say, *you're forgetting about the millions of people dying for a look at Hawaii*. Because when they'd lived there, her mom had called those people fools. She'd once turned blue trying to convince her mother otherwise. It was probably the angriest she'd ever been at her.

Her mother snatched the Barolo from Emma's hand and gave herself a generous pour in whoever's glass she was drinking from. "No, let's. Life doesn't go on and on, you know. You only get one shot at it. And your father and I worry that you are stuck living in the past."

She might have to update the angriest award.

"Is that why you think I settled on Oahu? Because of Michael?"

"Well, isn't it? It's the reason you left Paris."

"No, Mother, that wasn't the reason." It so was. Had it been Emma all along driving a wedge between her and her parents? Between her and Michael even? Unable to be herself?

"Well, what is it? You know you can always talk to us," Mother said leaning an elbow on the ancient marble island between them.

"Can I?"

"Of course."

"Why don't I feel that way?" She knew those words must have hurt. That wasn't her intention, and yet, the need to say them came from somewhere deep inside of her that she hadn't known existed.

TWENTY-TWO

MICHAEL

By the time the worst Uber driver in the history of the world dropped me at Dad's, I was a mess. I figured I'd spend the night after the flight from the Big Island making us a nice dinner and trying to salvage the rest of my stay. My father was barely functioning as a human three years after Maku's passing, and here I was wrapped up in trying to sort out my own happiness. That wasn't why I'd come, I told myself. I tried to make it stick.

"Hey, Dad!" I yelled as the door swung open and I bent to lift my bag.

No one was there. Three hours later he came back, slightly sunburnt.

"Been beach cleaning."

"Dad." He wasn't meant to be out in the intense sun like that, getting so overheated.

"I know. But I hate litter. I can't let it pile up like that." He tossed his hat in the basket beside the door and went to the kitchen to splash some water on his face.

"Maybe all the taxes you pay could go to getting some of that sorted."

"It's a complicated issue, son. Who pays, when, why."

"Doesn't sound like it should be complicated."

I poured him a cold glass of water from the cooler.

"How was your trip?" he asked before taking a long, shaky sip.

"Good."

"It's strange, you know. You were over there on Hawaii with Corey, and yet Corey dropped by here the other night." He looked out the window instead of at me.

"Did he now?" I tried to act like these words had no meaning, hiked up my shorts.

"Must have one of those teleporting devices." Dad turned back to me. I couldn't say if it was good or bad, the feeling of someone who knew me so well looking right into me that way.

"Definitely." I didn't look away. I wanted him to know I appreciated his kindness and understanding. He knew I'd tell him in time. I usually liked Dad's *laissez-faire* communication methods, except at times like this, when I needed someone to drag it out of me and possibly hit me with something.

WHEN I MET PATRICIA, I had literally been laughing with a fellow Polynesian, about our shared pet peeve: when someone in Boston asked us where we're from because they noticed we looked slightly "exotic." I'd told the guy, whose name escapes me now, "I'll say, 'Well, gee willikers, thanks,' in my rendition of a midwestern twang. They don't know what to make of that, which makes them uncomfortable."

"Good," Whatever His Name had said.

"Exactly."

That's when Patricia had walked up and said the exact

thing to him. Whatever His Name had cough-laughed, but then double-raised his brows and shrugged. Because she was hot.

We slept together that night. If I were the kind of person who dug down deep, I might say I was punishing myself or putting a face to many ugly things in my life and fucking them, but at the time I was not so deep. In fact, I'd really prefer never to think about that part of it.

She did a lot of the things that other girls wouldn't do. At first, it was non-exclusive. We'd go out to our separate bars: me on Comm Ave—beers and baseball, or Mexican and football, she on upscale Charles Street or the overpriced Financial District. At about two she'd ring me, and we'd go home together. It was nice, and easy, and sometimes I liked the way I had to tell whatever girl had been attached to my lips that I had to go meet someone. I could be a dick, too.

A chip, his roommate Frank called it. "You have a chip on your shoulder because you think you're different."

"I *am* different, you dick. And I'm glad. Who wants to be like you?"

But they were good mates. Did everything together, though they'd drifted since graduation. Frank made faces behind Patricia's back in the mornings, but he was in constant awe of her hotness. It was epic. And she had daddy issues, which signaled to us at the time, that she was good in bed—that was what people were always saying. But it really meant she was too consumed with me, wanted me to be everything to her, and if I were the right guy for her, I would have been dying to show her that was what I would be. But I wasn't.

At times I did my worst; it was mostly on a subconscious level. I wanted to push her away. But she wouldn't budge. We became a unit, in our way. And then the tables turned on me when Maku was sick—I probably deserved it for the way I'd been so cavalier about Patricia's needs—and *I* needed *her*.

She was there for me, in her way. Which wasn't my way, but she didn't, couldn't work that out. Patricia had trouble seeing around herself.

Still, I had my moments. Like some of the darker days, waiting outside the Kapiolani Women's and Children's Hospital, where even the name said I was useless, when I needed to feel that deep connection only a woman could provide. On one of those days, I went to a ridiculously pricey shop in Ala Moana Center and bought some tiny "fat" hoop earrings, which the woman had called "Huggies."

"Like the diapers?" I'd asked.

I was home, so she smiled and patted my hand. "Yes, Kukio." This stranger had comforted me more than Patricia ever had. I should've given *her* the earrings.

Instead, every time I saw Patricia wearing them—which was every fucking day of my life—I thought of shit, both literally and figuratively.

TWENTY-THREE

EMMA

Upstairs later, alone in her *pigeonnier*, at the top of a tower, she could see some gaping holes in her Hawaiian life. A meal full of people like this shined a brighter light on all the meals she ate alone on her sofa. Why hadn't she felt empty while she was living it if it was all so dismal and lonely? Was she holding onto the past? Eating her dinner with a ghost? Was her mother right?

Until she could work it out, she certainly wasn't going to say as much to anyone. Michael thought she didn't need him all those years ago, and her mother thought she needed him so much she screwed up her life. Was the truth somewhere in between the two? And what did it matter anyway if he was married to someone else? What she needed, stuck up here with her thoughts in this tower, was to be saved by a prince charming. Not the fairy tale kind, but the modern kind. The kind that could make her stomach tip with all the feels, show her she was still alive without Michael, could enjoy a heightened, bursting-to-the-seams experience with another man, if not with her cozy blanket. And the shaggy, blond Italian seemed like the perfect candidate.

But in the morning, she couldn't seem to muster the same kind of bravado. She knew she had plans with him later and the only feels she could muster were nervousness and stomach upset.

Her dream was fresh in her mind. She'd been at home, but it was a different home. And judging from the crowd around the breakfast table, she lived there with Michael and Patricia, whose nickname she had changed to Tiny Hoop Earrings, in the abbreviated: THE. Emma was sensationally jealous in the dream. She picked up THE's Honey Nut Cheerios and yelled, "This is not breakfast for an adult! This is not even breakfast for a child! It is full of sugar and you only think it's healthy because of the marketing people who put that idea in your head, you stupid, stupid woman!"

But she was the stupid woman, she thought this morning, looking out the tiny pigeon windows, with their delicate soldered handles. How lovely to think of curling a message around a tiny bird's foot and sending it off into the world, loaded with hope and expectation, unsure of whether it could even reach its target. She was the stupid, old-fashioned woman who had tried to be all the things she was meant to be and, in the process, fooled herself out of a life. *But look how independent she is!* Stupid, stupid woman. And she'd been so terrified of making another mistake with Michael that she'd only wound up screwing things up further.

She needed to think about Gianni. She needed to get into the mindset of washing that guy right out of her hair. Perhaps she could shock her body into a new life. One that had nothing to do with Michael. Or Hawaii for that matter.

Downstairs in the kitchen, her dad was clacking at the gleaming espresso machine. Within seconds he handed her a coffee identical to the one on the table in front of her mother, who sat alongside her. He served it in a small cup, without milk. The first sip was shocking, but she was in that kind of headspace and welcomed the sensation.

"How are you feeling?" her mother asked.

Familial controversy was not a Taylor thing and she was pretty sure her mother had as little idea how to proceed as she did. Were they even meant to be speaking to each other?

When they came out, Emma's words were as much a surprise to her as they must have been to her parents. "There might have been some truth in what you said last night."

"Thank you for saying that," her mother said, then took a sip of her coffee. "But I needn't have said them so harshly. I find these days I've been speaking my mind more than I'm comfortable with. But there is something to be said for it. Even when they come out as sloppy and unkind as last night. Probably, we could have done a little more of that in this family over the years."

Her father turned from the machine and smiled. Her parents were a well-oiled team. She'd had that with Michael, she couldn't help thinking.

When it was time to leave for Gianni's place, Emma bundled up for the walk to the "neighboring" property, which was nearly half a mile away. Her father had made a song list on her phone with dozens of his favorite Italian songs, so she hooked on her earphones and set on her way. The walk was cleansing and energizing. She passed a seven-hundred-year-old church on the other side of the road with incredible vertical architecture. She decided to duck in. The heart-rending desire coming off those statues was palpable. People hadn't changed that much.

She dropped some coins into the donation box and lit a candle. But for whom? It came to her in a flash: *it's for whomever that girl was in Paris all those years ago.* If anything had come clear, it was what had led to their breakup all those years ago. And some, if not all, of it had been her fault. Her blowup on the Big Island had cast that into sharp relief. She shut things down to seek comfort—at the cost of missing the big picture. She wasn't a changed woman, and she wasn't sure she wouldn't make the same mistake again, but at least she owned it.

She watched for a while as the flame flickered, sparked and danced in fits and starts. Eventually, it took a firm hold, which brought a deep satisfaction in her heart.

Where the street inclined, she climbed a worn stone staircase. At the top, she could see the whole town. It was like a time capsule, and she was lucky to have the opportunity to come here when she needed a recharge. She should take advantage of it more often. And she should take advantage of the available single, sexy male who'd invited her to his place. She still wasn't quite ready for that, but she'd cross that bridge when she came to it.

She turned to descend the precipice to the other side of the hill, where Gianni's property was. But then she recalled this was the cell phone spot where she could actually get reception. It had been so nice to be removed from all that, the complete turn-off of the constant screen refreshing to see if Michael had reached out or posted anything that might clue her in.

Still, she couldn't seem to stop herself from holding the phone aloft, her heart lifting at the illuminated three bars of reception. There were two Facebook message updates that quickly flashed and then faded before she had a chance to decipher them. *Two?* She braced herself.

We haven't seen you for a while at Leahi Health! Your next smoothie is on us! And don't forget Taco Tuesdays!

Her insides plummeted. But there was one more.

We should talk.

That one was from Candace. A relief, even if it was vague. Contact was good. It meant she was unhappy with the rift. She answered right away.

In Italy. Will be back on Wednesday. Lunch?

Because she couldn't help herself, Emma pulled up the Facebook app and cruised through her updates. Nothing caught her eye. She was just about to close it out when a photo jumped out at her. Michael. With Patricia. It was a selfie style shot, and it was clear by the position and crop of her arm, that she was the photographer. Michael looked serious—serious in love, or remorse, or something else, she couldn't tell. But there he was, as deadly serious as he'd been with *her* just days ago in a honeymoon suite on the Big Island, now with his wife. Now she felt justified for every over-excited, under-considered word she'd said. Why had she been blaming herself? He was *married*. She lowered the phone and looked out over the cliff edge again. What she saw down there was a giant world in which she was a meaningless speck.

She would have to screw her way to increasing the size and meaning of her speck. It was the only tool at her disposal, and the Facebook post had given her the fire necessary to ignite her into action. She was glad she'd seen it. Because otherwise, she probably wouldn't have been able to go through with it.

Gianni was up on a ladder that leaned against a peaked roof when she made her way through the stone entry walls of his property. Along with her dad's soundtrack soaring through her earbuds, and the image of Michael and his wife burned onto her retinas, the trees and walls and stone structures were even bigger and bolder and more powerful—Grimm's fairytale proportions that could grab and scrape her into submission.

Even in her negative state, it was clear the place was magical and would have a future of celebrity guests and top ten lists.

The completed twin of the building Gianni was atop of was

about forty feet away. Each was made up of a simple timber structure alongside a small original stone structure, which must have once been used for outhouses or root cellars or protection. The new builds were modern and clean. Mixed with the brick, they had a classic flavor that gave the place a distinctive look implying that this was how this place was meant to be.

As she approached, he was nailing in beams all by himself. She could tell there were other people that worked there because there were backpacks and water jugs amongst other tool kits.

It took him a minute to realize she was there. When he did, he finished the nail he was working on, pulled another from between his lips, smoothed a palm over the work, and then descended the ladder. As he leaned in for the two Italian kisses, her heartbeat picked up at the feel of his scruffy cheeks against hers. The scent of his aftershave didn't hurt. God, if she was after masculine, she'd certainly found it.

"You like?" he asked.

"When can I book in?" She could feel him looking at her mouth as she spoke.

"Nah, nah. Friends are always welcome."

"If you can put an extra-large sunken tub in this one, I'd be happy." Emma shrugged.

"Deal. Ready for the tour?" He lightly palmed her shoulder to guide the way.

The first stop was the kitchen of the larger stone building set aside from the two guesthouses, where he reached into a rack set above the oversized island and pulled out two huge wine glasses.

"The tour is much better with a glass of wine. The vineyards here are over three hundred years old. They belonged to my grandfather and his grandfather before that." The roots, the solidity blew her away. She wanted to at least taste what that was like.

He pulled the cork on a bottle that was half full and made two generous pours.

"*Alla salute.*" He handed her a glass, then clinked his into hers.

The wine was sharper than she was used to. But it opened itself in waves—a leathery hit, fruit, loam. She closed her eyes to explore the sensations.

"That's how we live around here." Was she crazy or was he giving off some vibes? She couldn't tell if that was just the way a gorgeous Italian man treated every woman, or this one in particular, but for once, that didn't seem to matter. In fact, it was probably better if she got the everywoman treatment, so she'd get used to what her life would be like now that she was once and for all done with love.

"Do you ever feel like you need a change?" she asked as he led the way back down the hall through which they'd entered.

"Yup. Did that once."

"Where'd you go?" Emma tilted her head to take him in, where he walked alongside her.

"New York."

"New York! If you can make it there, you can make it anywhere."

"That's what they say because they haven't been through Siberian winters."

"Have you?" she asked, her finger at her lips, where she'd felt him gazing.

"No. I came up with that when I returned home with my tail between my legs. People seem to buy it." There was a lovely crinkle at his eyes when he smiled.

They laughed.

"What really brought you back?" she asked.

"All this." He'd brought them to a brick courtyard, and he swept a hand at the structures and greenery around them.

"Did you like New York? I'm sure all the girls were head over heels for you." Now she could feel herself pouting to play into the attention he was paying her mouth.

"Eh," he said, shrugging. "I don't like to brag." He tucked the thumb of his free hand in a belt loop.

"Sure, you don't."

"In the end, it was too loud and too close, and it didn't sit right with me." Gianni shook his head.

"I know what you mean. It's very quiet where I live, too. I'm pretty lucky. And I love where I work, which takes my commute against the traffic, so it all works out well." As she said it, she knew it was true. There was more to her connection to Oahu than avoidance and fear. She loved the place, warts and all. She hadn't sincerely considered leaving since she'd moved back there. Surely that couldn't have all been down to Michael? She wasn't going to poke too hard yet at the wound he'd left. She'd have to wait for the inflammation to subside.

"Are you going to stay there? Your parents are so far away." He looked genuinely interested.

It was her turn to shrug. "We're a military family. You move with new opportunity, you stay the same person, you pack light, and you always carry a flashlight."

He nodded along with her, but his comment was skeptical. "You've got it all worked out."

"I do. More please." She held up her glass. "This wine is delicious." She noticed his was empty, too.

"Yes. But be careful. It can give you a bit of a headache. Americans, I mean. Italians, we're used to it." He smiled, his mouth closed, and reached out for her glass.

That was a challenge if she ever heard one. She saluted and he did that eye crinkle again. They made a quick detour to the kitchen and then took the hallway in the opposite direction. Emma's next sip was larger than she'd intended. When she stood to continue the tour, she had to hold onto the countertop to steady herself.

To his credit, Gianni pretended not to notice. But that didn't mean he wouldn't use it to his advantage, if he was so inclined, which, she reminded herself, she had no idea about.

He nodded toward another guest room down the hall and she followed. She ran her hand over the unfinished wood planks decoratively bordering the hallway halfway up. The suites still lacked many of the necessary furnishings, but she could see it all coming together. There was a huge iron bed in the middle of the room, with a Madonna painted in an oval on the headboard. But, like the new builds, there was a modern touch to some of the pieces.

"Where do you get all these newer additions?" she asked.

"Get them? I *make* them."

"Make them?"

"It's wood, it's nails. Finished. Been doing it my whole life. There aren't many furniture shops around here. Why do you think we keep each piece so long? It's valued. If you take care in making it, not like all this internet quick this and quick that, and online dating—I like you, I don't know you—and fast food, if you take it slow and do it right, it will last. Things don't move at a fast pace here—another thing Americans can't handle. We'll see how long your parents last." He smiled.

"That's a lot of opinions in one sentence. I wonder why Italians have a reputation for being condescending?"

"*Boh*. There's some truth to it. I can tell you see it, too." He smoothed his palm over the surface of a spare bedside table. The wood was naked, sanded to perfection, and its simplicity brought the eye straight to the Madonna on the headboard. His thoughtfulness and eye for beauty made him even more attractive—not like he needed any help in that area.

"How?" She was being flirtatious. Her normally pouty lips twitched as she saw his eyes watch them.

He squinted. "You know how. There's something about you, isn't there?" Or there was something he was projecting onto a woman he didn't know, because that was what everyone did with their fantasies. Just like she was doing.

Still, were there words that more deeply filled our needs? He was hot. It shouldn't have been difficult. And she was fired up from Michael's photo. No photos in all that time and then he chose to post that. Surely there was a personal message there for her. But when she closed her eyes and tried to picture what she would like intimacy with Gianni to look like, all she saw were replays of Michael. Fucker.

But Emma felt something on her lips, and to her surprise, her insides stirred. She didn't open her eyes. This was kind of wrong, with the Michael image still in her mind, and also the strange newness of this beautiful Italian man's lips on hers. His kiss was incredibly sensual, drawn out and savored. And that was a ridiculous turn-on. No anger fuel required, though there was plenty of that.

He put a hand at the back of her head and it nearly made her cry. Oh, how she needed that. She opened her eyes and forced herself to watch him watching her to distract herself from tears. He knew what he was doing. He pulled back, then kissed at her jaw. She shivered.

He backed away a few inches, looking seriously at her.

Emma couldn't think what to say, so she continued their conversation as if the kiss had never happened.

"Oh, my parents are here to stay. They've never said that about anywhere before. In fact, they've been saying lots of stuff they never said before." Her life was getting a kick in the ass that she hadn't asked for, and here were the consequences.

"At least that means I'll be seeing more of you." His hand

was at her hair, his fingers following a long wave all the way to the end.

She didn't look at him when he said that. Instead, she backed out toward the door. She wasn't sure why. But she knew how the penis worked. That would only make him want her more. Inadvertently hard-to-get was the best kind.

"How long will you be here for?"

"Just through the week."

"And then what?" he asked.

"Back to work." The words felt unreal, far-off. Emma couldn't imagine working at the moment.

"What do you do for work?" He reached her at the doorway, kissed her again, slowly, but just the once, then passed her and palmed for her to follow him down the soft-lit hallway.

"Why don't we concentrate on what we're doing here?"

At her question, Gianni stopped, then looked at her over his shoulder. Eyes, lips, eyes lips, his gaze darted between them. "Oh, I am."

She smiled larger than she would have liked, but his lips mirrored her own. As she followed him out to the impressive sitting room, with its massive blue velvet sofa, cut in a minimalist shape, the idea of work stuck in her craw. The last thing she felt like talking or thinking about was marketing, especially with someone possibly more averse to the technological and social norms of this modern age than herself. Still, she had a sense her *aloha* personal touch idea wouldn't even begin to satisfy the kind of personal touch Gianni was used to. She could tell the inspiration was making connections in her subconscious. Her brain was absorbing even as she tried to screw her way out of heartbreak. She was a true professional.

He took her hand and showed her through the rest of the room, all of which made incredible use of the combination of old and new, with strong pops of color and enormous gilt mirrors and windows with sparse coverings and imperceptible downlights to bring it all together. A great big geometric painting over the marble fireplace took her breath away. He finished the tour with the rooms she hadn't seen. Each bathroom was a work of art—ancient and timeless in the best way, care of travertine, more giant paintings, and minimalist fixtures, all complementing an incredible egg-shaped tub.

"This place is magnificent," she said.

"I'm glad you like it." He squeezed her palm, probably without thinking of it. Instinctively, she pulled her hand away. He pretended not to notice. Which was lucky enough, as she was already chiding herself. Couldn't she stop thinking of Michael for one minute? He was with somebody else. Married to somebody else. It was going to be a long, lonely life for her if all she did was pine for him. Of course, screwing this guy wasn't a symbol for her whole life, but it certainly felt like one.

They walked in silence for a minute, out of this suite and along the hallway to its neighbor.

"I'm getting hungry. Would you like some lunch?" Gianni asked.

"Sure." He briefly continued the tour of the last room, the enormous communal dining table beneath a high, beamed roof. The table was modern and sparse, the wood sanded back like the bedside table, this wood a pale honey hue.

"That table is beautiful. You are incredibly talented." Talent was attractive, and she felt honored to be so closely involved with it here. This time she reached for him. And he took this as an invitation, kissing her longer and harder, and then lingering at her ear in a way that made her quiver with sensation.

Now it was his turn to pretend it hadn't happened.

"Lunch?" Gianni asked, as if his lips hadn't just been on her skin.

And his hard-to-get worked just as well on her. There had

been no need to worry about her body cooperating. It was abundantly clear they were in on this together.

Back in the kitchen, he set about boiling water and pulling ingredients from a large pantry off to the side.

"What are we having?" she asked.

"Pasta. What else?" She saw him pile glass containers of various sizes into the crook of his arm.

Gianni proceeded to make the pasta, fresh. Gorgeous little gnocchi, which he finished off with a press of a fork's tines, speaking to Emma all the while and barely looking at his busy hands.

He put out some fresh bread, olive oil, and cheese on a wooden board that matched the style of the furnishings he'd showed her earlier. She was beginning to recognize his touch.

She stacked some cheese on a bread disc and found herself moaning.

"You like?"

"That's incredible," she said, covering her mouth with her palm.

"That's home."

Picturing the canal view from her window, she knew what he meant, even through the fog of drink and lust, and if she could feel like that about her home in this atmosphere, it was clear where she stood, at least on that front. But she'd file that for later. If she ever remembered anything about this evening.

"You like your food," he said.

"I like *your* food. You wouldn't believe some of the foods they eat in Hawaii." Emma played with the stem of her glass.

"Like what?" He lifted the lid on the pot to view the rapidly boiling water inside.

"You ever heard of Spam?"

He repeated the word, but the way he pronounced it *spom* made her laugh. Where had she heard that? It slammed into her brain with force: the couple she and Michael had overheard at the resort. He tipped the board of gnocci gently into the water.

She began to choke on her wine. Gianni reached inside a cabinet for a water glass, which he quickly filled from the tap and handed to her, with a gentle hand on her back. She gulped it down. Was the intensity between them being trampled over by her?

Once they'd established that she was okay, he said, "Tell me about this *spom*."

She breathed deeply to keep from laughing. "It's tinned ham."

"You mean, like from the war?"

"Yup."

"But surely they don't need to eat that now?"

"No, but they make special sushi pieces out of it, and they have it on the menu at McDonald's; it's everywhere." She held her hands out and grimaced.

"Okay, tradition. I get. But still, not most appetizing."

"Totally." What she left out was how much she loved it. "But not really *my* tradition."

"What do you mean?" he asked.

"Well, I'm not *from* Hawaii. I chose to go back there, but it was one of a dozen places I'd lived growing up. After university, I tried to think where would be the best place for me to settle. And my mind just kept going back to Hawaii."

"And this has nothing to do with the previously unmentioned romance?"

This again? And from an Italian man she was meant to be using to wash him out of her hair?

"No. I hadn't seen him in years by then."

"Who is this *him*?"

"Never mind. I don't even feel like I really miss him."

"Good."

"I just feel bad because of the unfinished business." What was she doing? She was ruining everything. "It was the place I knew best. I thought, I'm gonna put down some roots."

"I can understand that." He squeezed her arm and returned to the pot to have a look.

Good. Now she needed to change the subject before she'd quashed the whole idea of sex. Realizing how close she'd been to that made her realize how badly she wanted Gianni. And how deeply, in the moment, she didn't care why.

"You surf?" he asked, as he turned out the flame beneath the pot.

"Yes."

"Frightening, no? The power of the waves?" He removed the lid and carried the deep pot to the sink, where he had a strainer set to catch the beautiful pasta.

She watched the puffy ovals carried by the flow. "Sure." Fear was the reason she surfed. To remind herself that she had feelings, that she wasn't in control of life the way she imagined. No wonder she hadn't done it in so long. "Do you surf?"

He nodded, spooning the pasta into shallow gray bowls for them. "Been to the Basque coast a few times last season. The Costa Brava. The water is not so warm as your Hawaiian beaches. What's it like having the warmth all year round?" He poured over the bowls the fragrant garlicky sauce he'd been concocting on the small cast iron pan, pinched some salt, pepper, and parsley over the top, then picked them up, nodding toward the dining room. "Grab the wine."

She nodded and brought the glasses and bottle, following him. "You start taking it for granted after a while. Like it's just another sunny day. Something you'll never run out of. Like air."

In candlelight, they sat catty-corner at one tiny bit of the table, ancient placemats beneath their bowls and glasses. They looked like something from the Medicis.

"You are a realist."

They were silent for a moment, the candlelight dancing between them.

"We could use someone like you for this hotel," Gianni said. "I don't know anything about PR."

"I don't want to talk about work, but I'll say this: I think you're a natural. You know a lot more than you think. You'll have the paparazzi outside your walls in no time."

"But how does that all work? I need someone to pull it together." He spoke with sweeping hand gestures.

"It's your passion, your knowledge, your warmth. Those are all the things that a marketing person is going to try to recreate anyway. It's just that everything's on the internet these days, so we're working out all the ways to translate that with the new technology," Emma said.

Despite what she'd said, she told him a bit about the current work she was doing. Trying to humanize the inhuman, authenticate the inauthentic. "I gave them the old-fashioned *aloha*." She pushed the image of an enraged Candace out of her mind.

"Sounds a lot like Italy."

She smiled.

"People have been averse to live marketing in the past decade because it's not scalable."

"Scalable?"

"You can't increase the reach of your efforts without putting in all the effort again," she said.

"Sounds very mechanical."

"Well, it is, but I believe there's a balance. You can't get stuck having to do the same work over and over again. And you do need the proof and the data and the budgets, but it's more organic than that."

Something occurred to her. "Do you even have a mobile phone?"

He shook his head. "What do I need that for? All I need is some pigeons. Tie a note around one of their ankles, and in two hours, I get a response. Perfect."

They laughed. "So, that was you who sent me that note the other night? Well, the answer is yes. Yes, I would like to do everything you said."

There was that smile of his. Wicked. They were back on track.

"How come you didn't make it up for Thanksgiving?" he asked. "Isn't that a big deal for Americans?"

"I wanted to, but—"

"That sounds like the kind of but that has some romantic entanglement involved with it."

"No."

"Yes." He rubbed at his hair.

"Okay. You're good." She surrendered her palms.

His smile was wicked. "But you don't want to talk about it."

"Really good." She made a pistol with her fingers and pointed it at him with a wink. When she opened her eye again the room fluttered a bit. All of a sudden, that wine had gone to her head.

"*Che si fotta*." She knew the words: fuck him.

"I love it." And she did. She thought she'd ruined things by bringing him up, but the idea of Gianni slamming him was also appealing. Childish, but somehow sexy.

"Is it me, or is there an attraction between us?" he asked, leaning further back in his chair, his arms and legs spreading wide.

"It's just because I'm exotic," she said.

"Don't often get blue jean American girls in this neck of the woods."

"We're worth all the hype, aren't we?" She forked the last of her pasta and pretended his change in posture had no effect on her. "Do you think you'll live here or stay with your family?" she asked him. "It's a big place to knock around in all by yourself."

He smirked when she said *knock around*. She'd crossed her legs at the same moment, instinctively. The physicality was on track.

"Having this kind of place is really a 24-hour job. And until I have staff I can trust, I have to oversee it all. And on the other hand, if my family knows how much work I'm doing, by the hours I keep, then they'll be back here all the time to help. So, best I stay here. With the lights off." He smiled and pointed up into the darkness.

There were a few large candelabras that sat along the deep window sills, that she hadn't noticed until then. He brought one over and lit each candle, slowly. She could see the stiffness inside his jeans.

Yes, body, I hear you.

"You like?" He came over to her chair and gently nudged her legs apart with his knee.

Was she being ungenerous, or was this not the first time he'd given this tour in quite this way? In other circumstances, her instincts might make her question that, but now she waved the unwelcome thought away. This felt perfect for what she was after: a nudge, an awakening with no complications. And now that she felt herself physically reacting, there didn't seem to be anything standing in the way.

She nodded. He pulled her to standing and sat her on his lap, as if he'd read her thoughts.

This kiss had a life of its own. She couldn't have described its speed, style, or particular movements. It did its job and floated her off into its own dimension, one where she stopped thinking and just felt. And she felt good.

When he pulled away, his lips nearly touching hers, he

whispered, "Come. Help me make more of this pasta for you to take home. I'd like to teach you. I think you will enjoy it."

Gianni led her back to the kitchen, around to the workspace, which was floured. He reached up to a light switch, which he used to turn off all the lights except the pendants above them, which he lowered just enough for them to see the floured space. He used a dough-cutter to slice off a hunk and then cut that one into smaller bits, which he rolled. Coming behind her, he put the fork in her hand, laid his fingers over hers, led her through applying just the right pressure to the dough. All the while, he applied coordinating pressure from his groin into her backside. She barely knew what he was saying with his erection between them. Somehow, they finished pressing the tines into all the bits of pasta. She was breathless and desperate for him by then.

He refreshed her glass. She let out a huge breath.

"What about my headache? I thought you were going to watch out for me."

"I thought you were independent. All you needed was a flashlight." He shrugged one shoulder, replaced the wine bottle alongside the sink.

She smiled at him and accepted the plates he handed her this time, topped with two very chocolate filled dessert glasses to take into the dining room, where the massive table dominated the space. Approaching the seat he pulled out for her, she could see she'd missed the incredible, ancient parquetry across the surface. In the light of the extra candelabra, she could make out the detailed shapes of children, dogs, ducks, and trees in the woodwork. It wasn't a modern piece as she'd imagined. It was an old one repurposed carefully and lovingly into something even more incredible than the original. She vocalized the view.

"This table, in its former shape, was the first piece of furniture my great grandfather made. And my mother polished it every single Sunday. And when she brought it over here for me to use in any way I liked, I couldn't believe it. My mother is a stickler for tradition."

He laid out two placemats, their plates, proper silver cutlery, water glasses, brought out another bottle of wine with their glasses.

"And you're not?"

"Not in quite the same way."

"It makes the room. Cheers to us putting it to good use." Was that the next level of flirting? If so, had she just hinted she was going to have sex with him on this ancient table? And had his smile grown even more devilish? Likely, she was playing right into his hand. But *touché*, Gianni. That was exactly what she was after.

TWENTY-FOUR

EMMA

Gianni held out his fork for her to try a bite of fluffy chocolate dessert.

Emma leaned over—a bit too much, she nearly fell off her seat because she was well and truly drunk, but she caught herself—and parted her lips, letting him slide the rich mousse inside. Slowly, she closed around it and groaned.

When had she enjoyed a bite of food so deeply? If this is what he could do to her with food, she could only imagine what lay ahead for her. Maybe earlier, when she hadn't thought she could fuck Michael out of her hair, she hadn't considered just what an Italian man brought to the table.

In her weakened, wined-up state, she thought she'd worked out the missing piece. She also quashed that voice in her head that said she was being naive and not a little prejudiced. Shut up and screw the hot Italian man, she told the voice.

She hadn't noticed she'd closed her eyes until she opened them and saw him staring at her, grinning. Suddenly self-conscious, she licked at the corner of her mouth, where she felt the cold of some chocolate. His eyes dilated. She gulped. He kissed her, the taste of chocolate between them.

AN HOUR later there was yet more red wine while they relaxed on cane chairs in the moonlight, the air around them erotically charged.

In a silent moment they turned to each other. Gianni reached for Emma's hand and then yanked her onto his chair, atop his lap, so that they were both staring up at the stars.

"Are you ready to fuck him?" he whispered in her ear, in plain English this time.

He had so hit the bull's-eye so precisely it scared her a little.

"Yes," she found herself saying despite the trepidation.

She needed this. She needed him.

"How badly do you want to hurt him?"

"This badly," she said, and pulled her sweater over her head to reveal a black lace bra. The same one she'd worn for Michael on the Big Island in another life.

"Show me," he said, standing them both up and turning her to face him. Emma could feel him rigid against her. He pressed more deeply into her. She closed her eyes in exquisite desire. God it felt good. She could do the wrong thing, too.

And she moved in to show him, kissed him hungrily, breathlessly, deeply, while he undid the bra clasp and dragged his fingers around to her nipple, causing her to arch even further, adding pressure against his stiffness.

His fingers were all over her bare skin before they tucked beneath her jeans. She allowed him to slide his palm down her belly, down, to where she was wet with desire. When he pulled his hand out, she watched his thumb and forefinger undo her button, and effortlessly unzip her before he pulled down at her pants.

She enjoyed undressing him, pulling his shirt over his head. His chest was ripped and smooth. Her hands explored, her mouth followed.

"Fuck him," he whispered into her ear again.

"Yes," she said, and then he stood her up, to free himself from the confines of his jeans. Beneath his perfectly fitted boxer briefs, his erection was marvelous. Shivering, she touched him lightly there.

"That's it," he said. And this set her off. Soon they were completely naked, the blanket now over them on the lounge chair. He turned her onto her back.

"Fuck him," he said.

"No, fuck me," she whispered.

He groaned and did as she said. It was all sensation, all reaction, and she lost herself in it, completely. And when she felt her intense, pulsing release, he said, "I feel you coming," and then he did, too, and collapsed on top of her.

THEY LAY silent on the chair for a bit and both dozed off. A while later, they woke to the sun beginning to light up the sky.

He slipped out from beneath her and dressed.

"Let me give you a lift home," he said.

He handed her a helmet and they hopped on his Vespa.

Just when she was relaxing into it, he'd brought things to an abrupt end.

Emma felt vulnerable now. He'd been right about the headache. He'd been right about her need to exorcise Michael. It had felt amazing in the moment, but now? Now the comfort was beginning to wane. There was the satisfaction, the intimacy with Gianni. But there was also the stark reality. She still wanted Michael. She could have a lifetime of hot sex with strangers and she would still want him.

It was chilly on the back of the bike and she was acutely aware of his body between her legs, where she was still sore from his length. In many ways she felt like a teenager again. *Fuck it! Fuck everything!* But she'd literally done that, and now she was going home to her parents, much later than they would have expected her, drunk, convincing herself she could hide all her problems from them.

They arrived at her parents' place in ten minutes. Gianni cut the engine and stopped out front. She still couldn't believe they lived there—in a structure so old and elegant and strong. She looked up. The light was flickering in the den. Her dad was probably learning how to bake bread from scratch. It was so irritating how they could just go with the flow, start again, and enjoy every bit of their lives. And how she couldn't.

She was the only phony in the family when it came to that. But it was all starting to catch up with her.

"Thanks for the ride, the meal, the tour, the wine . . . the sex."

"You are very welcome," he said, kissing her in that erotic way of his.

"See you around," he said, as he started up the engine.

She saluted as he rode off.

EMMA TIPTOED into the sitting room where her parents watched television and read books, simultaneously, together but not together, in their own queer way. It was deathly quiet in there, except for a loud ticking from an old grandfather clock that was painted with saints in place of numbers.

Emma understood she was drunk and should go to bed. There was nothing else for it. All the same, she looked up Michael's number on her phone, typed it into her parents' landline extension, dialed the international code, and then his number, and heard the ring. Vertigo tore through her. What was she doing? On the fifth ring, his voicemail called out. *You've reached Michael Kavanagh, leave a message.* And so she did.

"Michael, it's Emma." That was a dumb start. And she didn't know where to go from there. *I fucked someone and he kept saying "fuck him," as if you were a presence in the room, and somehow you were. You* are?

"We need to talk. I want to hear your side of things. I want to know the truth."

Despite the rasp of her words, the obviousness of the time, she'd said more or less the right thing, she thought. And then she got a glass of water. Then another. And walked up to her tower to sleep it off.

TWENTY-FIVE

MICHAEL

Before I'd gone back home to pack and collect my things from the home I shared with Patricia, I let her know I was going to be there so she could clear out for a couple of days. She'd been cordial enough on the phone, so I figured things were going to be okay.

By the time I'd boarded the plane for Oahu, I was so relieved to be out of there, I half thought I would never return to Boston. The house was on the market. The fucking house I loved so much. I'd been so proud of that place. I had seen one just like it when I first arrived in Boston. It had been the night of a dinner at my boss's house, outside the city. There was steel and glass and stone, everything simple, streamlined, beautiful, daring you not to stare.

In Honolulu, houses were generally modest. There was just enough room for what you needed. If you were lucky, you had a great view to enjoy on your postage stamp-size lanai. But if you didn't, you took your beach chair to the shore and enjoyed it there, with three hundred of your closest friends and a butt-load of rotisserie chicken and kalua pork. People even brought rice cookers with generators. The world was your home. (Even if there was never anywhere to park in it.)

But this house said to me, *I will make my own world*. And there was something appealing about that, too. And at first, I'd enjoyed the novelty of the choices—light wood or dark? Which shade of white paint on the walls? Light fixtures, all of it. I spent a good deal of time on site, talking with the contractors, seeing how it all came together, even pitching in from time to time. There were more than a few nails, floor planks driven in by my own hands.

I thought I'd be satisfied there, feel, finally, that the world was coming together as I always felt it should.

But in the end it had merely been another wake-up call. I didn't belong there. The house began to embarrass me, as if everyone could see what I'd done, how obvious my desperation was. I could barely stand the sight of it.

None of this seemed to dawn on Patricia, who began devoting herself to the intricacies of soft touch drawers and Egyptian cotton so deeply that one day she'd come home to announce she'd quit her job. This renovation was too much work and she couldn't possibly do both any longer.

I'd felt sick at the idea of how completely she'd built her life around me. "Of course," I'd said, to anything she wanted. I owed her that. Though what I really should have done was stopped it right there. Strike two.

Instead, I did exactly the wrong thing. I started to check out Emma online. I examined the sparse photos and updates that were available to the public on Facebook—mainly photos she'd been tagged in through other pages—and finally, one night, clicked the friend request button. For months, nothing. I went home to my glass castle, checked whether she'd accepted, and tried to be in the moment. I'd chosen this life. There were plenty of people worse off. I should just be thankful for what I had.

TWENTY-SIX

MICHAEL

I was back with Dad for less than two days when I made the decision. I convinced him to leave the house and go to Rainbow Drive-In for plate lunches. This was a compromise for us because, on a Tuesday, I could eat the BBQ Ahi (a second runner-up to poke on my favorites list), while he carb-loaded on corned beef hash with egg and gravy, two scoops of white rice and a scoop of macaroni salad.

"God, this is good," I said.

Dad grunted. He'd lost weight. His belly barely covered his belt anymore.

It was a busy place and nearly every seat was full. Say what you want about Hawaii, but it's the most diverse state in the union, probably one of the most diverse spots on the planet. It's a mish-mash of everywhere and everything. I didn't quite understand how the food evolved to be some of the unhealthiest in the world, or why mashing cultures meant putting a scoop of mayonnaise-based pasta or potato salad (or both) and chips alongside two already generous scoops of rice. I didn't buy the story about extra carb loading out in the plantation days, because why not another scoop of rice, or noodles, or some Portuguese carb that was popular? Instead oily, mayo-slick pasta salad? Still, even those quirks I was fond of. And when no one was looking, I could demolish such a plate.

"I'm going to be coming home, Dad. For good. I'm sure you've noticed Patricia didn't come with me, and that's because things didn't work out with us."

"Because you still love Emma." He forked a mound of glistening macaroni salad.

I was startled. "Excuse me?"

"You love her. Maku said it all the time."

"Maku did?"

"She didn't like to meddle."

"Yes, she did."

"Okay, maybe she did. She was vocally strong in an obtuse way about wanting you to meet the right woman, settle down, and give her three grandkids. But she was afraid to push you *specifically* when it came to Emma, or any girl. Not with the hard time her family had given her when we were getting married. She was afraid she was putting her own hang-ups on you because your relationship was so intense, so consuming, like ours was." His voice faltered and I did him the favor of looking away.

"I didn't know they gave you grief about that. I thought it was a joke. You're all so close."

"I know. But once upon a time, that wasn't the case." He wiped his mouth with a flimsy paper napkin and then squashed it in his fist.

"I'm a moron."

"Yup." Dad took a long sip from his fountain Coke.

I told him Patricia and I were getting divorced.

"I'm sorry to hear that. You'll let me know if you need anything."

I nodded and that was the end of it.

"It'll be good to have you back, Son."

Now it was his turn to look away.

WE DROVE the long way home, taking a detour around Diamond Head Crater. Dad liked to listen to Hawaii Public Radio and Derrick Malama was talking to a woman who worked at The Doris Duke House, Shangri La, which offered tours through the Honolulu Museum of Art. My mind went straight to the time I'd gone there with Emma's family once. I'd never even known it existed, but the place was breathtaking, filled with incredible Islamic treasures that some people thought were bizarre or even inappropriate, although I hadn't seen them that way. Every room was a treasure trove, and I remember the four of us being swept away by this millionairess' life, laughing at the scale of the money and the scope of Duke's.

Symmetrical but not perfect. If anything looked too perfect, the artist would put a flaw in purposely. Finding your paradise and staying there forever was the theme underlying the whole day, and we'd all been swept away by it.

"Bet it was easy to find paradise here," Emma's dad had said, referring to the glamour and indulgence of it all. But he, too, giggled and went goggle-eyed at the ornate ceilings, the floor-to-ceiling glass on the open-air sitting room looking out over the ocean.

After, though, at a Chinese lunch at Little Village, Mr. And Mrs. Taylor had begun cracking jokes about how Honolulu was as far from paradise as a person could get, and they pointed to homeless guys wheeling themselves across the street, overfilled rubbish cans, graffitied buildings, and burned out cars on the roadside.

Emma had gotten angry. "Mom! Dad! You're being incredibly rude! Michael is from here. This is his home."

"Come on, Emma! Michael, those things are all true, aren't they?"

"Mrs. Taylor this is not a perfect place, that is true. But it is paradise to me. I've got everything I need. My family, the surf, and Emma."

I remember squeezing her hand so hard that I thought I'd hurt her. She swallowed audibly and her dad changed the topic to sports. In that moment, though, my words were perfectly accurate. Everything had been paradise—not perfect, because nothing is. But it was my Shangri-La all the same. And boy, had I fucked it up.

When I pulled into the driveway and cut the engine, I heard my phone signal a missed call and voicemail. It was Emma.

"Michael, it's Emma. We need to talk. I want to hear your side of things. I want to know the truth."

It was time to make this right. I knew just what to do.

TWENTY-SEVEN

EMMA

Hers was a long, fitful, and dehydrated sleep. Emma dreamed of Gianni saying, "Fuck him," and realized exactly what she had been doing. Whoever said to go for meaningless sex after a heartbreak was either trying to look much stronger than they were, or hadn't really been in love the first time around.

All that the encounter with the perfect-for-the-big-screen man who knew exactly what to do and exactly what to say ("fuck him"—she was still cringing at her intense reaction to that) had done was make her realize she'd not properly mourned the blow-up of this second chance with Michael. Probably she never would, because even now she felt herself tucking this idea back out to the periphery of her mind.

She tried to concentrate on the chemistry with Gianni. It was an incredible sexual experience, fucked up as it may have been. Every inch of her body had felt electrified, and she'd delighted in the novelty of exploring each bit of his perfect body. There'd been pleasure and orgasms. And if that was all she'd ever known, Gianni would have been more than just a notch in her lipstick case (*yes Candace, I'm using your favorite phrase, from your favorite song, even though you hate me, because I miss you dearly and want, more than anything, to walk up the hill and call you right now so you can help me through this*).

But it wasn't all she'd known. She'd experienced this level of chemistry bound up inextricably with love and history and a sense of (clearly mistaken) complete knowledge of the man behind the nearly picture perfect (if not for the jagged shiny scar from a surfing incident over his right nipple) chest.

Emma reached for her water glass only to find she'd already drained the last sip. Her head throbbed and her mouth had passed well beyond dry to a place where every surface was sticking to every other surface. She tried her best to ignore it all, took one last look at the bright, mid-day sun outside the tiny windows of her *pigeonnier* tower, pulled the blanket over her head, and prayed for sleep. Or a cross-continental message around a pigeon's foot, or, if she was being honest, Michael.

TWENTY-EIGHT

MICHAEL

There were available plane tickets to Rome. Of course there were. But they were $2,500, and not for business class. Fine. That didn't matter, even though I was about to be divorced and lose half of everything. I would relax with a couple of scotches and a movie and try not to think too much about the fact that this was not going to be easy to put right.

Three strikes. Everyone knows that. Just in case, Dad reminded me about it in the car ride to the airport.

"Don't fuck it up," he'd said, as I closed the door. Dad was a man of few words, but when he chose to speak, he didn't mince them.

"*Mi dispiace,*" said the female flight attendant, "but the entertainment system appears to be down, sir." She'd known what I was going to ask. The TV probably hadn't worked in weeks. Weren't flight attendants at least supposed to be hot if they were going to deliver terrible information?

Irrelevant.

Okay. Sixteen and a half hours in the air with nothing but my own completely fucked-up thoughts, but that was better, probably. I could sort through the debris of my life and come up with a plan of action.

TWENTY-NINE

EMMA

She'd spent all of the day before in bed. The hangover was her main excuse, but the experience with Gianni had been a kind of exorcism and she'd needed to put a full stop on things for the moment.

Sure, she'd spent some of the day feeling deeply blue, but mainly she was planning, trying to sort out where the holes were —because she felt she didn't really have all the information where Michael was concerned, and she needed to get it before she could give up the ghost. Because, despite how angry she was, she still loved him, and wanted there to be something real and forgivable in Michael's excuse, and she needed to ready herself to hear it.

But, finally, it was time to get up and get started. She carried down from her room the remnants of the cups of coffee and meals her parents had kindly brought up to her. Had it been that obvious that she needed space?

Her parents sat side by side on the sofa, enjoying coffees. The fire was glowing in the large fireplace opposite, and the whole scene was perfect. They had made the right choice settling here.

"Good morning," her father said, and made his way to the coffee machine to sort her out.

"Good morning. I'm out of the tower."

"Sounds like something from the War of the Roses."

"If I'm being honest, and I am trying to—" She made eye contact with her mother and forced herself to hold it. "It felt like that, too. Much more so than any fairytale princess. Before I came here, I reconnected with Michael."

Her mother did not hide her shock. Nor did she try to look pleased.

"And now it turns out that it's most likely not going to work out. And I'm pretty devastated."

Her mother's face changed, softened. Of course she couldn't understand about romantic heartache. She'd met Emma's father at West Point and they'd been together since. But by now, surely she could recognize the symptoms.

Her mother didn't come so far as to embrace her, but she did extend a hand, which she used to stroke at her arm in a way that made Emma's skin crawl, but she appreciated the sentiment. How would her mother, or anyone else, know she disliked such rubbing if she'd never told them?

They had a coffee and then she was off to Gianni's. She needed to say something to him, though she wasn't sure what. But this time she wasn't going to let that stop her.

"I'm off to Gianni's now," she said.

When her mother smiled smugly, she didn't correct her. Not every ugly truth needed to be outed in one fell swoop.

AS SHE BEGAN the walk to Gianni's, her old sweaters weren't so much comforting as they were stinking of mothballs.

The smell was wreaking havoc on her day-two hangover. Did everything have to turn ugly eventually? This walk never could. And within a few moments, she lost herself in it—the cypresses dotted hillside, the ancient rooflines, church spires, crumbling walls.

What did she want to say to Gianni? Because when she woke up that was one thing she'd been certain she must do: confront him. But now? Now she felt thankful to him for dredging her out of whatever she'd been buried in. It had been dramatic, erotic, wrong even, but it happened to be just what she'd needed.

GIANNI WASN'T EXPECTING HER, but she could tell he wasn't surprised when he spotted her from midway up his ladder, as if he'd noticed her before he'd turned her way. Perhaps he was more in touch with his animal side than most. Four other crewmembers were there this time, wearing the tool belts she'd seen discarded on her last visit. They were painting some kind of finish on the wooden structure. She stood for a second, watching him finish up some hammering.

She hadn't accounted for the tug in her abdomen at the sight of his smile. He was ridiculously attractive, she'd not exactly forgotten so much as left it out of her narrative from her day in the tower yesterday. It shouldn't have made a difference, except that his territorial body language toward her did have an effect. It eased the anxiety. They had shared the most intimate act two people could, and for someone who didn't easily open up, it meant more than it should.

Emma enjoyed watching him descend the ladder. There was something of a *deja vu* to the whole thing and she couldn't deny that seeing his body, in front of these people, when she'd seen it and felt everything underneath his clothes the way she had, was satisfying and made her feel a smug sort of proprietary right over him.

The customary European two kisses, which he drew out long and slow, gave her an inkling of his own view of the other night. There was no question she could have a repeat performance if that's what she wanted. Was that why she'd really come here? And without a *plan*?

"*Ciao, bella.*"

There was more abdominal tugging that Emma was desperately trying to ignore while Gianni called a few things in Italian to the workmen and then took her hand and led them to the house.

Couldn't she get some words of wisdom out of him and *also* enjoy his body one more time?

Though it was only 10:00 a.m., he poured them glasses of the house red. There was something of the expert in him. She could see this, and though it should have turned her off, it only really underlined her hunch that he knew what drove men, and that he might have some way of looking at this Michael thing that swung her way. And that—she realized—was why she'd felt she needed to speak with him.

But when he handed her the glass, he did so by coming up behind her, so that she could feel him already stirring in what she pictured were his beautiful black underwear beneath those old jeans.

But was that guilt stabbing at her chest? Was she serious? Michael hadn't even responded to her message, and it had certainly cost her to write it, to come to the thoughts even.

No. No. She was morally bound to be true to Michael with the decisions she'd made about her feelings and intentions with him, even if he hadn't been open with her in the past. And even if—should he ever answer—his response would be that he had strayed from his wife and that they were going to try to make it work now.

She shimmied away from his groin and made her way to the other side of the island.

He smiled. It was his confidence, that's what she needed to get behind, because it reminded her just then of that smile Michael had given her on the plane ride back to Oahu. There was a message there, but she hadn't been able to translate it. Likely, though, Gianni could. If only she could resist the temptation to do something *other than* what they'd done the previous night, she felt sure Gianni could help her with the most painful, most significant problem in her life.

THIRTY

MICHAEL

Fucking Italians. The plane circled the landing strip for forty-five minutes. By the last fifteen I was beginning to lose my cool and make snide comments for the benefit of anyone who could hear.

This did not make me feel any better. The waiting had deepened the anxious feeling that had seeped into and then flooded my body in the last twelve hours without a fucking distraction (yes, I'm aware how many F-bombs I'm dropping), that I had completely fucked up my already unlikely second chance with Emma. Why had I been so set on surprising her at her parents' house in a grand romantic gesture? What I probably should have done was answer her voicemail. By now she may have given up on me entirely. In the birthplace of the Casanova. What had I been thinking?

I hadn't been. I'd been going on instinct. This was what I'd always done where Emma was concerned. It was what had fucked things up in the first place back in Paris. Because instinct could easily get caught up in ego. And it was impossible to pick the two apart.

But I'd had years to tease them apart, and here I was making the same mistake again.

By then I pictured her in the arms of some eyebrow-combed Italian man in a shirt with too many buttons undone, telling her all the things she wanted to hear. And why wouldn't she let him, after how things went with me?

THE PROCESS SPED up once I was on the ground. Thankfully, I hadn't checked any luggage. I passed right by those suckers waiting for their bags when I made my way out to the taxi line. There was one ready for me, a well-gelled male at the steering wheel, trying to out-smell me with his cologne.

Fine. I was ready to alpha-male myself into the necessary role after all that on-air emotional turmoil. I felt free and now I was going to get things done.

"*Dove?*" he said. Where to. I'd memorized some phrases from the in-flight magazine in the absence of any other distraction. It was probably how they kept their circulation numbers up.

I felt a smile make its way to my lips. And then I rattled off Emma's parents' address, which was an hour out of town. I enjoyed witnessing the displeasure on his face. One point for me.

It had cost me to get the address from her parents. After recalling that time after the Doris Duke house, I had no choice but to track them down. There was no obvious telephone number on the internet and so I'd had to use the only email address I found, which was a shared one: TomandKarenTaylor263@gmail.com.

Dear General and Mrs. Taylor,

I am not sure what, if anything, Emma has told you of our current activities, so I will be as respectful to her privacy as I can in this communication. She and I have recently come to share that we made a mistake all those years ago—one that neither of us has been able to get past—splitting up. And we have come some way toward rectifying that.

But I have once again thrown a grenade in our path by being dishonest. I did not tell Emma about my ongoing divorce, and I'm afraid someone else has made her aware of my ex in a way that has caused her to think we are still together.

I will make no bones about the truth at this juncture: too much has been lost in doing so in the past. I know you both have never been thrilled about Emma's relationship with me. But I understand about caring for Emma's wellbeing, and I'm sure that's what drove you, whatever your impression of me. And I do believe that you would approve of the adult version of me (despite what I've just confessed to above), because the truth is, I've spent all this time becoming the kind of man that would make Emma happy in every way possible. My greatest mistake is that I did not share any of this with her, nor, to be honest, with myself, and that I have wasted many years of Emma's, my ex's, and my own life in the process, when a little humbling honesty would have been a better bet.

But I reveal my true self to you now, in asking for your help in proceeding to make things right. If you will forward me your address, I plan to surprise Emma and, if she will allow it, begin our shared future together—in the way we both discussed a few days ago.

Despite the ridiculous number of times I refreshed my inbox, I did not hear from them for several days. I won't share the unkind thoughts I had of General and Mrs. Taylor during that time. But they made things right, and I was willing to put that in the past (though perhaps snide thoughts would still be acceptable).

22 *Via delle Rose, Bracciano*

It was a sparse response and I took it as an endorsement of the sort they were capable of making. Which was enough for me.

THIRTY-ONE

EMMA

She began her long, convoluted story about what had happened with the man of the "fuck him" fame. And once she had, she saw something shift in Gianni's demeanor. He must have finally realized she was devoted to another.

This did not mean he wasn't trying to maneuver his way around that. But that was just his alpha-male instinct. Beneath that, he was dedicated to the cause. Because if there was one thing an Italian male was known for, it was loyalty to family and friends. And the Taylors were part of that now. And, for once, being a Taylor didn't seem like an alien concept to her.

To outside eyes, it would appear that Gianni was still trying to sleep with her. But he listened and advised in a shockingly honest, insightful way. And by the end of her ride home on his Vespa—even with her body snugged up to his solid ass—she felt she understood why Michael had done the things he had, even if he was still married. And she was willing to forgive them—if he made it right. And if he wouldn't answer her text, she was going to get to him however she could.

. . .

"WHY DON'T you come up and have a look? I think you'd love the beautiful tiny pigeon windows in there."

"I thought you wanted only this Michael. Now you are asking me up to your bedroom?" Gianni smiled like he was only teasing, and yet that teasing still had a sexy air. "I think it's time for me to go."

She caught the sincerity and meaning in his gaze. "Yeah, you're right. I probably couldn't trust you up there anyway."

"Of course."

She handed him the helmet she'd been wearing, and he put it into a compartment at the back.

"Gianni! *Ciao*," her mother said, executing the double kisses like a local.

"*Ciao*, Karen."

"He's just going," Emma said.

"Oh, that's a shame," her mother said, looking like the cat who ate the canary. What was that all about?

Emma shot her a look. Her mother shrugged. Gianni leaned in and kissed Emma below her ear.

Gianni climbed on his Vespa and looked up to Emma's bedroom. "A beautiful woman, all alone in a tower. It's like a fairy tale, no?"

Was he trying to get one last shot while the going was good?

"To tell you the truth, it's been quite a good place to think." She wished her mother would give them a moment. "The world looks puzzling when you can only spot bits of it out those tiny windows, like there's a bigger picture out there you have no idea about."

Gianni started up the engine and rolled back to release the kickstand. He raised a hand and drove off.

Emma and her mother stood in silence, watching him disappear over the hill.

Later, Emma stood in front of the smattering of tiny windows, once again puzzled at the world below. She watched a taxi make its way down their side of the hill and pull into their driveway.

She'd know that back, leaning into the taxi's trunk anywhere. Michael. She said the word out loud.

Before she knew what was happening, her mother was outside greeting him with the double kisses. Emma pried open one of the tiny windows. She could hear her mother say, "*Ciao, Michele*! Come and rescue your princess up there in her tower!"

Emma shot back from the window before they could see her staring down at them.

After Michael followed her mother inside, she couldn't make out any conversation. There was only a low hum making its way up and inside to her.

She sat on the bed thinking what to do, but she was too slow.

"Up there," she heard her mother say from the foot of the stairs. Then she heard Michael's footsteps. He was coming up.

All Emma could think was how sorry she was to have shared such intimacies with Gianni. Michael would find the idea of her speaking about him to Gianni repulsive, and she couldn't blame him given the whole *fuck him* thing.

"Please don't let my family know I shared any of this with you," she'd said to Gianni earlier.

"What we shared was between us." He'd kissed her on the cheek, and she knew he meant it. But she felt uneasy about it.

The next moment Michael was on the landing, then through the door, wearing a black leather jacket over a surfing T-shirt. He shut the door with his boot. She could barely believe he was there. He threw his small carry-on case down on the bed and lifted her off her feet.

"I love you," he said, gazing into her eyes, Emma still in his arms. He lowered her onto the bed, clearing his bag onto the floor, and kissed her in exactly the way she'd dreamed the previous night.

He was desperate, as desperate as she was. They were trembling and sloppy, and their clothes were not even all the way off. He had to be inside her it seemed, as much as she wanted him to be.

When he entered her, they moaned together, like two halves of a whole finally together. He was larger than she'd remembered. She was off on that pure sensation of him and who she was with him, and in moments she felt her body shatter and tighten in a rush of release around him. He followed suit and pulled her on top of him, holding her so tightly it seemed he was using his arms to say the words he couldn't yet.

But speak they must. She understood that, though she wanted just to lie there, the tiny puzzle pieces of the sky purpling with the dusk, the world not all figured out but a beautiful mystery that she could feel, truly feel, in every nerve ending of her body. The truth, she feared, could never be quite as satisfying.

THIRTY-TWO

MICHAEL

Lying in that crazy tower room with all the itty-bitty windows, I couldn't stop squeezing Emma to me. I needed her skin against mine. In all the time I worried I'd lost her again, this is what I'd imagined, and now I understood why.

We'd wound up in this situation because we hadn't given each other the benefit of the doubt and because we hadn't been honest with each other. I wasn't about to make the same mistake twice. And that meant getting the truth out in the open.

"I'm here because I love you, and I want to explain the truth of what's happened with Patricia." I saw Emma flinch at the sound of her name. I hadn't spoken it before, but I needed to get this out properly now. Patricia was a real person, and I'd seriously fucked her over because of how much I loved Emma.

"I want to hear it," she said. "All of it." She pressed herself in even tighter against me

I began with how things had started casually between

Patricia and me, how they'd intensified around Maku's illness and death. Emma was crying as I told it. She knew how much I loved my mother. It was good to share this loss with her. I remembered feeling Emma's absence keenly at that time. That hole probably had more than a little to do with rushing into things with Patricia.

As soon as I thought it, I knew I should share that with Emma. And I did. More tears. I really was a terrible son of a bitch.

I dragged my finger beneath her eye, wiped her tears.

"I love you, Emma, always have. There is no one in this world for me but you."

She tried to speak but tears choked her words. Her face turned angry and I knew what it was—she hated crying. And here she was doing it in front of me. It was adorable, but I wasn't about to say so. She'd fucking hate that. I gave her the respect of turning away, looking at some imaginary speck through one of those tiny windows that immediately drove me crazy—to see only part of the whole; it was a form of Italian torture. No wonder their economy was in the shitter. Still, the place had an undeniable charm and calm that added something intangible to the exchange between us.

"I am only a full person with you, Michael. I have always known that. And it terrified me to need you. Which is why I must have acted that shameful way to you back in Paris all those years ago . . . and why I was so furious with you on the Big Island. I was finally accepting the truth of that, and then I found out—I thought I found out—that you'd betrayed me."

"You're right. That is exactly what I did—but not in the way that you think. I'm no longer with Patricia, but I should have told you everything about her. Instead, I found it better to pretend it had only ever been you and me, that I hadn't wasted so many years for us, for Patricia. It was cowardly.

"I'm in the process of divorcing Patricia. I'm giving her the house, more than half of my money. I owe her that, at least. But she's having trouble accepting the reality of us being over. She's always suspected I still loved you, and I don't know how she'll react when she finds out. She can be quite motivated, detached from guilt. She isn't a person to feel sorry for anything."

"Then how do you explain the photo on your Facebook feed of the two of you together?"

"What?"

"You don't know?"

"I never go on Facebook, unless I have to organize an event or send out a message to everyone at once. Or try to reach out to you."

"Here," she said, and reached for her phone before letting it drop to the bed. "Wait. I forgot. There's no service here."

"Good," I said. "That's better. Whatever ugly lies are on there, I need you to believe me. I haven't seen her in several months."

"You expect me to believe she doctored a photo, or, I don't know, put up a photo from another time claiming it's from now?"

"Yes. She's very good at denying reality. Which is exactly why she was able to marry me even though I loved you."

"Oh, Michael. How did you get yourself into a situation like this?"

"I don't know. It's seriously fucked up. Not exactly alpha-male behavior. Probably why I was ashamed to tell you about it."

"Why do you and I always think we have to put our best face forward for each other? That never works in the long run. It's time for us to be open and accepting of each other—warts and all," she said.

"You're right. But please don't ever say *warts* again when we're naked in bed together."

"Deal. See? That was a good start." She kissed me on the eyebrow. What a spot to kiss me. Like she loved my eyebrow. Which, in that moment, I felt she did.

I smiled. A real, natural smile. And it felt fucking great. "Come here," I said, and pulled her to me, kissing her long and slow on every bit of her body I could think of.

This time when I was inside of her, it wasn't frenzied. It was deliberate. I was in control. Her body was mine, just as mine was hers. When I came, it felt like signing in blood on the dotted line.

We fell asleep in each other's arms, and when we woke, there was one thought I could not get out of my head.

"And Guido—"

"Gianni—"

"Whatever happened with Guido, you keep that to yourself. I don't want to know. Ever. You and I followed a long winding road to get here. But what matters now is that we're here. Just you and me from now on." *And I will try not to think about smashing his face into a wall every time we come and visit your parents.*

I would not let her go again.

THIRTY-THREE

MICHAEL

The plane ride had been bliss. I splashed out on business class because if there was ever a time to do it, this was it. If I didn't use my money Patricia was going to take half of it anyway. Emma and I had talked over plans for my return to Hawaii. I was going to move in with her right away. We didn't want to waste any more time.

Emma and I had shared an Uber to Kailua and the driver dropped her off first. I'd felt hesitant about letting her go, as if it had all been so perfect and if we parted ways somehow I might fuck it up.

But I managed to watch her disappear behind her door and let the driver take me to Dad's house. We had some omelets for dinner and then I crashed. Woke up after eleven then next day to find Dad was gone. I figured I'd go to the supermarket and then prepare a nice meal for the two of us while I explained where things stood with me and Emma.

"Dad, I'm home!" I called, laden with four paper grocery bags in the no-handles style Hawaiians still tolerated.

"Darling!" I nearly fell over. It was Patricia, making her way from the kitchen to the foyer. Was this some *Fatal Attraction* playbook she was following?

"What are you doing, Patricia?"

"Your father is in bad shape. I'm here to help."

My poor dad, who liked entertaining guests less than he liked colonoscopies, emerged from the kitchen with a murderous look, which for him meant a faint smile rather than a medium (angry) or small one (kind of annoyed).

"Hello, Michael. Look who's turned up." Despite what I'd told him at lunch the other day, Dad would certainly never question Patricia about why she was there.

"I've got something I've got to do down the street," he said, which was complete bullshit, and let himself out. Nicest man on the planet. She was lucky Maku wasn't here.

I walked to the kitchen to get a drink of water and think for a second.

Patricia followed and while I filled glasses for both of us, she snaked her arms around my back.

"I forgive you," she said. "You'll come home and we'll make it work."

I shook my head, lowered the glasses onto the table and said, "I told you. I'm not in love with you, Patricia. You can't tell me you're going to stay with me when you know that."

"Well, the thing is, I'm pregnant."

THIRTY-FOUR

MICHAEL

I couldn't believe she said she was pregnant.

Maku taught me how to treat women, so I didn't say anything that might make the situation worse, but I was skeptical at best. We hadn't had sex in a couple of months. Patricia would have known sooner, and she wasn't exactly the kind of woman to hold something like that back.

"Your dad's so happy for us," she said.

My jaw dropped.

"If we're having a baby, I will support both you and the baby always. But let's make this official. We're going to the doctor right now to take a proper test."

I could see a tempest brewing inside her skull. I'm not going to lie. I was frightened.

"You marry me when you don't really love me, then you come back here to go on vacation with *her* to the Big Island, where you never took me, by the way, and then you want to accuse *me* of lying?"

"Hold on." I raised a palm. "How did you know I went with Emma?"

"What does that matter?"

"Patricia. How. Did. You. Know?"

"Technology. It's rather ingenious, really. I remotely installed a spying app on your phone and another on Emma's phone. When I saw that you were together using the tracking feature, I sent you a text saying I was coming to Hawaii, knowing there was a good chance she'd see it. If that didn't work, I had a few other tricks up my sleeve. Like my access to your Facebook account."

The photo. That was how she'd posted it.

I felt my fist tighten, so I stepped back, closed my eyes and took a deep breath to calm down before I answered.

When I opened them again, I said, "Doctor, now. Let's get in the car."

"I'm lying! Fine! I'm not pregnant. But it's your fault! This is what you've done to me! I wanted to have adorable Asian babies!"

"Listen, I am sorry. I take full responsibility for the failure of our marriage. There is no one to blame but me. But I can't take that back. *And I'm not Asian*. All I can do, all either of us can do, is try to pick up the pieces and make things right."

"I don't accept that." She sat down and crossed her arms in a huff.

It had been an emotional week. The last thing I felt like doing was dealing with her. I collapsed onto one of the bar stools and let my head drop into my hands. "Let me take you somewhere."

I decided we'd ride bicycles to the beach. I could burn off some anger and we wouldn't have to talk, as the path was narrow, forcing us to ride single file. It would give me a chance to gather my thoughts.

It was strange being on Maku's bicycle. I raised my eyes in an apology but knew that wouldn't hold much water. It was probably better that she wasn't there to see how badly I'd screwed up my life. It would kill her anyway.

The pedaling uphill was hard work but I was glad for the effort. My anger earlier had scared me. I needed to calm down and concentrate on what I could do now to move forward in the best way.

There'd been a lot of new construction over here. People around here liked to complain about change, but I didn't think it was as simple as all that. Things changed. Just a look at my Maku's funeral tattoo on my arm could attest to that. Despite everything, it was good to be back.

I stopped at Duke's, as good a place as any, I thought, since my mind was drawing a blank.

"No, let's continue up the hill. You've always talked about that special place you used to go at Lanikai. Let's go there." She looked genuine, and this gave me hope that maybe we could finally end this civilly.

"Okay," I said, and hopped on to lead the way. I didn't need to look behind to see that the view was having an effect on Patricia. Maybe this had been a good idea. Despite the homeless man sleeping under a tarp, the worn-out shelters, and the overflowing rubbish cans, it was impossible not to be affected by the place. I should never have left. I should never have made Emma's test at whether she wanted to so pressured. All these years she's been back here, living our life. But without me.

I pulled into the second parking lot, which was inexplicably overtaken by five matching pastel VW buses, and led us to the post where I'd tied this bike more times than I can say. I didn't think I'd done enough planning about what I was going to say, but it was as if my mind was stubbornly refusing to go in that direction. Thankfully, what it had been considering led me to the right place all along. Again, thank you, Maku. Listen to your *naa'au* she always said, referring to the small intestines, which Hawaiians believe to be the seat of thought, intellect and affections.

While I locked the bikes, Patricia was winded and drank from the Hydro Flask with the World Surfing League logo Maku had given me for Christmas a couple years back. It felt like a sign.

I led us to my favorite spot, the same place I'd gone to with Emma the other day and so many other days. Our spot. But when I passed the high sand dune, I could see there was a large group in a circle of Tommy Bahama beach chairs there, having some kind of event. Great, I thought.

But when I looked around the circle, I nearly fell over. There she was. Emma! She was eating a plate lunch with a bunch of hipsters.

THIRTY-FIVE

EMMA

Back at home, Emma's mind whirled with the incredible resolution to her decades-long screw-up with Michael, which as it turns out, had impacted all the other facets of her life. She was so excited that she'd begun to worry she was too happy, and surely she'd over-inflate from all the happiness and burst like a balloon.

They'd spent the night apart and it frightened her how difficult that had been. She'd kind of expected him to text or call her overnight, but he hadn't. She wasn't trying to get into a petty battle of will, but she couldn't bring herself to be the one to do it. Being honest with herself about the vulnerability of missing him this much after less than twenty-four hours scared her enough. Giving into it was a bridge too far, even for the new Emma.

And anyway, there was work to think about. The pressure was on to please D.N.E. She knew their account meant more than enough money to give her the new department and a couple of people to go along with it.

The team that had been assigned to her campaign and the clients had all sat down in that same conference room, and as her speech began to accelerate, she wished she had some CBD tea, she wouldn't lie to herself about that.

"We all know the keys to marketing: listen to what your customer wants and show them you'll deliver it. These days everyone's talking about creating 'communities' and delivering more than anyone expects. Yes, and yes. But it must be relevant. And unique." She went on to explain how they were going to accomplish this in our 24/7 culture with their offline campaign. She spelled out the pitfalls to avoid—like trying to be all things to all people. And what to concentrate on: scarcity and exclusivity.

The guys were hooked. Their eyes were glued to hers. And so were Sarah's. She'd done her homework. The only thing missing was Candace, but she wasn't going to allow herself to think of that in this moment.

"The bottom line is, we're too busy looking outward to remember that the reason people want what we're selling in the first place is because it's awesome. And we're going to remind them.

"Now, to put my words into action, we're going on an excursion. Here in Hawaii, yes. We're attracting world-class chefs and hipster boutique hotel chains, but that's not our core. What we do best is the simple plate lunch."

She smiled with a promise of delights to come and extended an arm toward the door, which opened to two beautiful raven-haired young ladies, not in kitschy hula garb, but authentic tailored muumuus, ruffles along the neck and shoulder line, done in a modern fabric—light, breathable, filmy. They were breathtaking. The girls handed out leis made by the most celebrated local lei makers, in the bright pink, white, and red colors of D.N.E.

In a caravan of impeccably restored pastel Volkswagen buses, they traveled to the same beach where she'd had that amazing first day with Michael nearly a month ago. There were ten Tommy Bahama beach chairs arranged in a circle, where everyone sat and ate Spam masubi appetizers and plate lunches from Styrofoam containers. Mai tais were done in old-fashioned brown tiki glasses.

"This is incredible," said the head marketing contact, Ron, "The Ronald" Frisch. "My girlfriend never lets me eat like this."

"And the good thing is, all the frying is done with coconut oil, which everybody knows is a good fat! And all the coating is done with brown rice flour. So, it's actually healthy! This place even offers brown rice, but the truth is, this white rice is a special high-protein high-fiber version grown right here on the islands. The science was completed at the University of Manoa. All the best of tradition with all the best of innovation—exactly what we're going to show the world about your brand. It's more work. It costs more, but in the end, the ROI is triple, so there's no question of the value."

"You are really impressive, Emma. Are you sure we can't poach you to come and work with us in-house?"

"That's very flattering, Ron."

"*The* Ron."

"*The* Ron. But Hawaii Nei is my home."

"Well, the offer stands. But I wouldn't want to leave here, either."

It was all going swimmingly. Emma tasted her chicken katsu dipped in tonkatsu sauce, and it nearly melted in her mouth. "Yum," she said.

Candace was to her right, keeping a neutral face.

They still hadn't spoken, but Emma knew Candace had handed in her resignation. She didn't know exactly why, but bits of strange conversations were coming back to her that were starting to make more sense, and of course, she was confident her CBD meltdown at the big meeting had been a catalyst for whatever had been brewing in the background.

"I know, this kalua pig is incredible. Don't tell me this one's healthy," said The Ron.

"Some things shouldn't change."

They both laughed, and when she threw her head back, she saw Michael with *her*—Small Hoop Earrings. Suddenly, everything around her went quiet except for the whooshing of the sea in her ears.

THIRTY-SIX

MICHAEL

"This? This is why you brought me here? To throw *her* in my face?"

"Calm down, Patricia. I didn't know she was going to be here."

Wait a minute, it was she who'd suggested we come here!

"Sure! You expect me to believe that? You Asians are so cruel!"

"I'm not Asian!"

"Polyn-Asian, whatever!"

I took a deep breath. I felt my fists tightening again and I needed to calm down. Who cared if she got my culture wrong now? Hopefully, after the divorce, I'd never have to see her again.

"Look, fair enough for you to be upset, Patricia. I know Italians have bad tempers." Let's see how she liked the stereotyping and prejudice.

"I'm Greek."

"Same thing, whatever." God, it felt good to dish out some of her own medicine.

How had I married her? I kept blaming it on Maku, really, but perhaps somewhere, if I were honest with myself, I knew I was running away from here, toward someone who loved me—now, I realize, it was toward someone who loved me too much. Someone who needed me and came right out and said it. Well, perspective is a motherfucker.

And all these years later we found ourselves here, Patricia's huggies catching the sun at Kailua Beach Park, so that I could try to finally make her realize we were not going to be together. Only, I hadn't known how I was going to actually accomplish that. She'd suggested the beach, and as soon as she said it, I knew it was the right place to put an end to things, finally. Though I didn't know exactly how, I just felt that at this beach, where I'd enjoyed some of the simplest, most clearly happy times of my life, I'd work it out. And then Emma—the woman who I'd somehow convinced to trust me even though I'd fucked up so badly and things looked so terrible from her point of view—showed up. There was no question how this would look to her.

Patricia knew I could outrun her, which was why she went for a different tactic.

"Emma!" she screamed, through a curled fist, as if she had a megaphone. It was one of her superpowers. She'd hushed a noisy club in the same way more than once.

Everyone turned around, including the beautiful ladies serving drinks to Emma and her crew, and of course, the crew itself, which I now realized was her huge work meeting. She hadn't mentioned it was going to be here, a key piece of information, but I wasn't in a position to be accusing anyone of withholding details. The guy next to her grinned like this was just the Hawaiian experience he was hoping to have. Moron.

"Don't," I said.

She didn't even look at me.

"You can have him!" Patricia said. "I can tell you all of his favorite positions. He loves it when my legs are up in the air. And then of course, you'll be sucking his dick—a lot!"

Did she *want* me to hit her? I'd never been closer. *Never hit a girl. Never hit a girl.*

The hipster douche in the chair next to Emma said something to her that I couldn't hear.

Emma shook her head.

Damned if I was going to let that guy save her. I'd get Patricia out of here and beg for open-mindedness from Emma later. Anything else in front of this work thing was just going to make things worse.

I left the bikes, picked Patricia up and carried her all the way home. Halfway there she stopped screaming obscenities and went limp. She might have even fallen asleep. Five minutes before we turned the corner to Dad's block, she told me she'd been cheating on me.

"It's your fault, obviously, since we never have sex anymore."

I put her down and kept walking.

She followed after me.

"Aren't you gonna say something?"

I wouldn't give her the satisfaction. I knew she'd been saving this for a last-ditch effort to get a rise out of me.

"I'm taking you to the airport. You will sign the divorce papers when they arrive."

I could see something flag in her. She was done.

We were silent most of the way into Honolulu to catch her flight, but when I turned onto Nimitz, off the highway, she said, "You should not marry someone you don't love."

"I know that." I grabbed for her hand. "I am deeply sorry.

You, on the other hand should not install tracking devices on people's phones."

"It worked, didn't it?"

I didn't answer. This would not be the topic our final exchange. I would get a new phone, a new number. If Emma ever spoke to me again, I'd do the same for her.

I was happy to see the back of Patricia, and if that meant I had to endure a hug, one final scene, and the dirty looks of more than one *tutu,* I was up for the punishment. My own grandmother, if she were alive, would laugh if I told her.

THIRTY-SEVEN

EMMA

"Candace, we really need to talk." Emma tried to sound natural.

The meeting was over and the D.N.E. guys were tucked safely in their hotel until this evening. Then Emma would bring them to her favorite Kailua restaurant, Over Easy, where a wonderful band she stole from La Mariana's for the night, would play Old Standards Hawaiian-Style, the way they'd been doing at the classic tiki bar for decades, handing out roses and all.

Candace was clearing out her office, and she surprised Emma by nodding when asked if she could come in.

"Yes, we do."

"I'm sorry—wait, huh?" They both said exactly the same thing in unison. Which was an excellent icebreaker. They smiled and Emma let her come in for a hug, which was something she normally would not allow. Candace was a hugger and she knew it made Emma uncomfortable. This was an excellent hug, though. She even felt one of those ghastly tears escape her eye. But she blinked quickly, before Candace could see.

"Felt that teardrop on my shoulder," she said, raising her chin. "You go first." Candace rolled her palm for Emma to start the details of her apology.

"There is no excuse for what I did to you at that meeting. You made a point of asking me quite a few times not to do something like that to you. I didn't understand why, but I should have respected that. And I'm sorry." She didn't blame it on the CBD because that would have undermined the apology.

"Actually, there is an excuse for that: CBD tea," Candace said.

Emma jolted back in her chair. "How do you know about that?"

"Ms. Chloe? I talked her into giving it to you. She'd noticed you'd been off for a few weeks and I explained to her about Michael, and how I was afraid you'd fuck it up again. Which was true. But she gave it to you on the wrong day. The day of the meeting."

"Let me get this straight: your way of helping me was to *drug* me? That is a crime that people can go to jail for!"

"It does sound pretty bad when you say it like that. Though, this isn't so much like drugging someone as giving them a really great chamomile tea. You have no idea what proper drugs feel like." Emma could not hide her shock. "But hang on. If you're that angry now, let me say the rest of it because I think it's going to sound even worse."

"There's more? You've been this mad at *me,* and there's more?"

"The blanket rubbed with stinky cheese, the torn nightgown, the bitter chocolate? All me. I did have your best interests at heart. I wanted to shake you out of your comfy cocoon and really give this thing with Michael a proper chance."

"Candace! How could you?"

"You have no idea how rare what you guys had was! You

have no idea how badly you pine for experiences like that when you're up all night with two vomiting kids, then have to make yourself presentable for work, then fail to be as amazing at it as your best friend who got a full night's sleep, which is a terrible kick in the ass because you and your husband have decided that if you don't get a promotion and a raise to go along with it, you just can't keep working, because with the cost of childcare and how much you make, you're actually *losing* money." The last word barely came out. It had taken a lot for her to admit to this. She had done some crappy stuff to Emma, but how could Emma not have seen how desperate her friend was?

"You know I don't like talking about my real problems. I just like to make jokes about stuff that isn't really bad, like poopy diapers, while I force you to bare your soul so I can pick it apart properly."

Now it was Emma's turn to reach for her.

"I do know that," she said. "But if I've learned anything with this whole Michael thing, it's that we must be honest with the people we love—even if it costs us to do so. And, also, I am so glad that wasn't actual vomit on my blanket."

They smiled. Candace and Emma packed up her desk while she spilled the details of what had been going on, how, in the end, she realized she was only trying to succeed so hard at work because she needed to make enough money to cover the childcare, to prove she had worth, when really all she wanted was to stay home with the kids instead of splitting her attentions.

"Now, that's enough brutal honesty on my part. Let's make you uncomfortable now. What in the world was that with Michael today?"

"What? You mean you haven't meddled in that part of it?"

"Again, I'm very sorry. I took advantage of how well I know you and forced your hand."

"You definitely overstepped. But you were right. I nearly let Michael go again. I nearly didn't accept his friend request. Without those sneaky, underhanded boosts of yours, I'd probably have let it all slip through my fingers again."

"I think you should look at this as an opportunity to put it right. Because it sounds like, from everything you said, that Michael probably has a reasonable explanation for appearing with that vulgar, though quite beautiful woman—"

Emma grimaced.

"Well, I'm not going to start lying now. Try to remember she felt desperate, and the things you yourself have done in that frame of mind."

"And you! Boy, you are really trying to make me into a proper adult, aren't you? Trial by fire. I feel for those kids of yours."

"Honestly, I think my job here is done. You've come pretty far—especially if you're willing to forgive me. I can't even believe how I treated you before Thanksgiving. I took out all my frustrations on you. And you're the last person to deserve it."

"I thought you were done talking about yourself."

"Seriously. You're my lifeline, Emma. I am quite ashamed of my actions."

"I haven't been too proud of myself lately, either. But we can both change that now. Can't be everything to everyone. Maybe just be true to yourself and take it from there."

"ALL FIXED?" Candace said, wiping her hands like she'd finished her project.

"Of course." It felt so good to get back into their sassy banter.

"Great. Then one last question: Did you do anything I would have done over in Italy?"

"Candace."

"Did you do any*one*?"

"Stop."

"If you asked for my advice, I would have told you to screw a hot Italian guy. You know that.

"I have no idea what you're talking about."

"Don't tell me you screwed this up. Do you know what I would do for a chance to screw a hot Italian guy? And if you're going to be with the same man for the rest of your life, now's the time!"

She leaned back. She was set on being honest, but not this honest.

Candace held up a palm and shook her head. "Don't worry. You don't have to tell me. I *know*. Just like I know you're all fixed up now from the way you're doing that manic nodding thing."

Emma finally let herself deflate. Her body seemed to dissolve onto Candace's desk chair.

"You think it's hard now? Well, wait until it's five years from now, you haven't given Michael a chance to explain, and then you finally realize that even by bedding a hundred Italians, you can't sweep this under the carpet."

"What is this with the sweeping under the carpet? Nobody sweeps anymore, and why in the world, if you were already doing all the hard work of sweeping, would you then just dump it under the carpet instead of emptying the tray in the trash?"

"Exactly. When it bites you in the ass—"

"I'm definitely not sweeping anything that's going to bite me in the ass," Emma said.

"You cried in front of me." There. They were even. She'd given what Candace desperately wanted, something she abhorred. And Candace knew it. She could already feel them getting onto more normal footing.

"Don't you dare say that again. And if you ask me to call you Aunty Candace I'm going to clock you. But Candace, nothing behind my back anymore. Okay?"

Candace nodded. It was so good to have her back. If Emma had to play up the things that made her friend feel good and useful then that's what she was going to do.

"Now I *know* my work here is done."

"Sure, as long as I don't need another dose of that tea to get me through this confrontation with Michael." She cocked a brow and shrugged.

TURNS out the tea idea was too good to resist.

"One of your special brews, Ms. Chloe," Emma said, with all the blame she could muster.

"Ms. Chloe knows what you need."

THIRTY-EIGHT

EMMA

In another story, Emma would have sworn off Facebook. She would have declared publicly that she never should have accepted that request. That it was the worst idea she'd ever had. That she'd known it could all go badly wrong, but she'd done it anyway. That she wasn't going to look at his profile ever again. She'd turn off all the alerts so she wouldn't be tempted to peek.

But Candace, the drug-pusher, the cheese-smusher was right. Emma would regret that path forever, and probably irreparably screw up her life in the process. She'd sworn from here on out she was going to be honest with herself. And just as she'd always thought she and Michael were two halves of a whole, she had to treat him with the same respect. Was this recklessness, this instinct to do things that were so dangerous to our well-being baked into every single one of us? If there was a thing as love—which she knew first-hand there was—then perhaps that was the one thing that could drive us there.

THIRTY-NINE

EMMA

Emma had received a text message from Michael after she drank the CBD tea and had weaved her weary feet quite a ways along the winding route to Michael's dad's house. She didn't feel any different than before she'd drunk the tea, but perhaps, since this was not the first time, it wouldn't feel as dramatic.

What happened earlier is completely my fault. Patricia did not take news of my relationship with you well and I've just dropped her at the airport. There is nothing between Patricia and me. Nothing has changed from what I shared with you in Italy. I am incredibly sorry for what happened on the beach at your meeting. And I hope there is a way you can forgive me because all I want in this whole world is you.

OKAY. She hadn't needed a second to consider her response.
Okay? Just like that? Do I have the wrong number?
No. You have exactly the right number. All I want in this whole world is you. There's no point in having the same conver-

sation we already had in Italy just because a messy situation got messier. Neither of us is going to let this chance escape us this time. I trust you.

There, she'd crossed the bridge, made herself completely vulnerable.

God, you are an incredible woman.

I know. You're a lucky man.

Listen, I'm in the middle of something here for you. Is it okay if I swing by your office tomorrow?

You mean I'm not going to get to see you tonight? (For me??? What is it?)

You might be able to talk me into it. (And I'm not telling)

If you come over, I'll be wearing nothing. (Now will you tell?) There; that would get it out of him.

An excellent argument. Done. I'll see you at your place. Six? (Still not telling.)

I'll be there. Naked.

I might be early. And then you'll find out the secret sooner.

Emma smiled. When it was right, and you've messed it up for ten years, maybe it could just happen overnight like that.

THE NEXT DAY, after an incredible evening with Michael, during which he'd decided he was not going to tell her the secret, but managed to distract her with all kinds of successful tactics, she was using a big legal pad to start a departmental establishment to-do list when her messenger pop-dinged with a note from Candace. It was such a welcome sight.

Just wanted you to know there was nothing in your tea last night. I called Chloe and told her you needed to accomplish your happily-ever-after with Michael all on your own.

Just when she was thinking she was actually grateful for Candace's meddling, and also how over-the-top her phrasing was, Sandi beeped through the intercom. and said, "The Ron is on line one."

She tried not to panic. Taylors do not panic. She knew better than to ask, *What else could go wrong?*

"Hello Emma. Ron here. I'm just going to get out with it."

Oh no.

"We do our research, too. People who are happy in their home life do a thirty percent better job at work. So, we're glad you sorted that out. Besides, I'm friends with Michael on Facebook so I was rooting for you guys."

Of course he was.

"So-*o*? I bet you had some amazing make-up sex after that."

"The Ron?"

"Sorry. I was just feel so comfortable with you. Part of your *ohana*."

I wrote on my list in big capital letters: CREATE BOUNDARIES.

"What can I do for you, Ron?" she asked.

"*The* Ron. Well, seeing as you've gotten together with Michael, I was kind of, well—"

"Come on, Ron, we're *ohana*."

"Okay. I'll just come out with it. Do you think that Patricia girl would be interested in me?"

AT 1:00 P.M. she got another buzz from Sandi.

"Surprise prospective client," she said.

"What? Showed up at the office without an appointment?" Emma said. She hadn't even had lunch yet.

"He said he had something more important than an appointment."

"Tell him I said to make an appointment."

"Hold on."

After a minute, she came back. "He says there's something heavy in his pants and he needs to give it to you."

Was this just inappropriate day, or what?

"Is it Michael?" Emma said.

"I'm not allowed to say."

"You'd better send him in, and kindly tell him to refrain from speaking that way in this office again."

The door opened and there was Michael, his black sunglasses perched atop his head, *aloha* shirt resting gorgeously on his muscled shoulders and chest.

"You might have misunderstood what I had Sandi tell you," he said, getting down on one knee and pulling from his back a black velvet box hinged open to reveal a stunning engagement ring.

She caught her breath. "This is why you should leave the communications to me."

"If you marry me, there won't be any conflict of interest in my hiring you, will there?" Michael asked.

"I'm sorry. Say that again."

As he moved to hold the ring out, his mourning tattoo from Maku flashed out from his sleeve. He caught her looking at it and wrapped his free fingers around both of her hands. "She loved you as much as I do."

Though Taylors don't do tears, she made an exception.

"*E male'oe ia'u*; Marry me."

"I could work it out from the context."

"Is that a yes?"

"'*Ae*"

He raised his eyebrows. "This is why I knew I needed to marry a Hawaiian girl. She knows the word yes."

"I'm not Hawaiian."

"You are. You're *kama'aina*. And I'm not talking about the discount."

"I can't get a family discount?"

"I love you, Emma. Your home is here—not just in Hawaii, but in Hawaii with *me*."

He pulled her from the chair, onto his knee. Cradling her chin in his free hand, he kissed her. He stood so they were eye to eye. "Now, please do me the honor of wearing this ring," he said, sliding the round, glittering diamond onto her finger.

The perfection of the moment was surreal. *Could this all be happening?*

"Yes." He seemed to read her thoughts. "This is real. Late, but worth waiting for. So, I believe the word you're looking for is *yes*."

"Yes. Definitely yes."

He let out a huge sigh, as if he wasn't as confident as he'd let on.

She leaned in to kiss him again, then paused. "Hang on," she said, and turned the legal pad back to the first page. She crossed out "no working with *ohana*."

The buzzer rang again. "Um, guys," Sandi said. "Should I get off the intercom and give you some privacy now?"

She went back to the words CREATE BOUNDARIES. And underlined it. Twice.

FORTY

EMMA

The next morning, enjoying a coffee with Michael on her couch, Emma's phone dinged with a message. It was right in sight on the desktop and impossible to miss. It was from Patricia.

Congratulations! You deserve each other, you sweeping-under-the-carpet losers!

"You didn't want to have a conversation," Michael said, "but I probably should have told you that Patricia hacked your phone with a tracking device, too. She's bought this crazy spy stuff off the internet."

"Details," she said, tossing a palm.

Michael picked up the phone. "May I?"

She nodded.

He carefully placed it on the floor and smashed it beneath his shoe.

"What is with this sweeping under the carpet thing?" she said, as she helped him pick up the shards. "See people pick things up when there's a mess. This is why people need your marketing firm—there is a serious lack of originality in this world."

"But wait. How did you know that's what I would do with my career?"

"Because I know you. And I love you."

"Oh, I like the way you say that," he said. Michael looked her straight in the eye, moved in so that the tips of their noses and every bit of their bodies touched. He kissed her like the embodiment of her idea of them: two pieces finally coming together. And then, with their lips still touching, he said, "I love you, Emma Taylor, and I can't wait to make you my wife."

"You don't say that so badly yourself."

Their smiles grew simultaneously, lips touching. She reached around and pulled his head in closer still. "Finally," she said, "this is home."

"It always has been your home," he said. "You win."

"By the way, if you know me that well, you're never going to let me get away with anything again, are you?"

Another joined smile, more kissing. "Depends on what you're trying to get away with," she said.

He leaned in, caressing her hair, and kissed her passionately.

"That, you can always get away with."

He kissed her again. "And that? Can I get away with that?"

She nodded.

He kissed her neck, then lower, and lower still.

"And that?"

"Let me just stop you there. I'll always let you get away with any of that."

"Now that's a happily ever after," he said, carrying her into the bedroom.

THE END

AUTHOR'S NOTE

Reviews are crucial for authors these days. Please share your experience by leaving a review on the site where you purchased this book, even if it's only a line or two.

For a free copy of Daniella Brodsky's novella, My Sizzling Second Chance, sign up for her readers' group by clicking here or visiting her at daniellabrodsky.com. You'll get access to more free books, launch information, and lots more insider bonuses.

ABOUT THE AUTHOR

Daniella Brodsky is the Australian/American author of novels published by Penguin, Random House, and Simon & Schuster, most recently, *VIVIAN RISING* and most famously *DIARY OF A WORKING GIRL*, which was adapted for the screen by Disney, starring Hilary Duff. She also had a long career as a journalist and made a name for herself with *THE GIRL'S GUIDE TO NEW YORK* nightlife, back when she didn't need a babysitter and a disco nap to stay out past seven.

Daniella has taught fiction craft at the ANU, James Cook University. A native New Yorker, Daniella has lived in North Queensland, Canberra, Honolulu, Washington D.C., and Sydney; she teaches creative writing at James Cook University and at her Captain Cook Studio. If you're looking for domestic suspense, check out her pen name, Dan Noble.

www.daniellabrodsky.com.
There you can learn about new releases, giveaways, and sales by signing up for her reader's group.

Copyright © 2019 by Daniella Brodsky

All rights reserved.

This is a work of fiction. Names, characters, places, and incidents either are the product of the author's imagination or are used fictitiously, and any resemblance to actual persons, living or dead, business establishments, events, or locales is entirely coincidental.

This eBook is licensed for your personal enjoyment only. This eBook may not be re-sold or given away to other people. If you would like to share this book with another person, please purchase an additional copy for each recipient. If you're reading this book and did not purchase it, or it was not purchased for your use only, please alert daniellabrodsky.com and purchase your own copy. Thank you for respecting the hard work of this author.

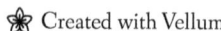 Created with Vellum

YOUR NEXT READ . . .

Keep Calm and Perfect Your Smolder
Book 2 in The Flame Series
by Daniella Brodsky

Chapter One
Maggie

"So who are these people we're eating dinner with again?" Reg looked at her as if this was brand new information he was inquiring after.

She'd told him twice but he'd been fiddling with his phone while the taxi waited at an endless red light, and she knew he hadn't been listening. She wasn't sure he was listening now, even though he was looking right at her. Later, he'd probably say she'd never told him their names. There was no point in arguing. He was hopeless at remembering details like names, birthdays, appointments.

That's why they were running late now. He'd been at the gym and she'd been pacing the apartment, trying his mobile to no result. When Reg sauntered in with a podcast turned up so loud her eye began to twitch, he stopped before he'd closed the door to answer a text and hadn't even noticed her standing in front of him with crossed arms.

He jumped when he saw her, and in the process dropped the phone he was using for yet another text message.

"Maggie! Why are you sneaking up on me like that?"

"Reg. I've been ringing you for an hour. We have that dinner with Florence from my work tonight. I put it in our Google calendar and on the calendar on the fridge. We spoke about it on the phone this morning."

"God! I hate calendars! Why do we have to go out on a Friday? It's been such a long week. And you didn't—oh, there, twelve missed calls? A bit much, no? What are they, Kennedys?" He sat on the woven bench and yanked at his shoelaces while she tried not to think how his sweat was going to stain the rattan.

"Please just get ready Reg. I've texted them to let them

know we're going to be late, but we were meant to be there in ten minutes. It'll take us at least triple that to get to the harbor."

"If we live in Paddington, where the best restaurants in the city are, then why are we going all the way to the end of the city?" He pulled his shirt over his head and let it fall on the bench beside him. He put the stinky trainers on top of it and left it like that. The running was slimming him down too much. Reg was naturally fit and now he was losing whatever bulk his chest had. And she'd really liked that bulk.

"I will tell you again in the taxi, but for now, please go shower." Thankfully he made his way down the hall. In front of the laundry room, he stepped out of his pants and kicked them close to but not *in* the hamper.

Maggie bent down to pick them up and recoiled at the soaked nylon.

"I don't know what to do with myself," he started to sing as he fiddled with the shower mixer and steam billowed into the hallway to destroy the sleek hairstyle she'd brushed, ironed, and smoothed into obedience earlier.

They were going to the Darlinghurst eatery because of the tasting menu. She and Florence were in the food biz. They were on the planning side these days, rather than behind the fry pans, but they both endlessly went on about getting back to their cooking roots. Neither of them had discussed practicalities, and usually there was wine involved in their oaths to do so, but Monday morning saw them both at their desks, planning and researching, rather than in the trenches.

She wasn't unhappy at Five Dinners, Done!, the meal delivery company taking over Australia, but she wasn't exactly happy either. Except when she spent time with Florence. They'd been promising to do this dinner thing for at least two years. And now here they were. Rushing, stressing (at least *she* was), but Maggie promised herself she'd calm down in the taxi so she could have a good time with her friend.

It would be great to take their friendship to the next level. And Florence's boyfriend, Lionel, was meant to be fun and exciting, according to Florence anyway. Maggie couldn't help thinking his name promised the opposite. *Lionel? What kind of name was that?* Something from a children's book about a wiley lion, it stuck in her craw.

He was in the military, so at least they'd have something to talk about. Maggie had grown up in a military family, and had worked on Fort Bliss for five years before she'd emigrated to Australia because of he who would remain nameless. But that was a long time ago, and surely she could go over those times without showing any signs of distress.

Reg used a card to pay the cab fare and it took forever. The driver had to reboot his payment system twice. She itched to use the emergency fifty she kept in her purse, but she knew that would piss Reg off now. He never carried cash and sorely resented it when she was prepared and he wasn't.

Fine. She'd walk in ahead.

The restaurant was in touristville, right at Sydney Harbour, with floor to ceiling windows overlooking the bridge, the quay, and the Opera House. As she climbed the stairs two at a time, she peered out the pristine glass to appreciate the view. It never got old. Sometimes she rode a ferry just for the purpose of appreciating it. It was like a little visual reassurance: *yes, you got it right coming here.*

Reg would catch up. The glamorous woman at the hostess stand asked for her name. "Maggie Jones," she said. "Table for four. We should have two people here already."

"Yes. You're very lucky. We're not really permitted to seat parties until all the guests have arrived, but *Lionel* was so persuasive, I let them." She shrugged, like, *who could resist him?*

Maggie hated him already. Which was unfortunate, as she'd pictured the four of them renting adjoining cabins on the South Coast and grilling steaks and snorkers over a campfire—even if Lionel's face was out of focus in the images.

"Let me take you." The woman's cascading blonde waves were picture-perfect. They swayed as she led Maggie.

She looked back, but there was no sign of Reg. Good. Let him sit there for an hour watching the taxi driver reboot the credit card device. If he needed her, he'd ring, surely.

How many nights had she spent listening to his friends drone on about financial jargon she couldn't even decipher? The one night she proposed to do something with *her* friend and he had to go out of his way to ruin it. She wouldn't let him. She happened to believe we were each the master of our own fate.

Still, she tried his phone as she followed the hostess's mesmerising hairdo around the winding dining room. He didn't answer.

"Maggie!" It was Florence, and she got the same punch-in-the-gut gratefulness she always did at the sight of her. Florence was waving her down frantically, as if she had been afraid Maggie would never actually show up. She wouldn't sell Reg out, but she wanted to.

Her friend ran over to her and her dense corkscrew curls, which she'd let hang loose this evening, blocked the view of the table she'd come from.

"I'm so glad you're here! They've given us the most amazing amuse-bouche while we were waiting! We'll have to get them to bring you one. I cannot wait for you to meet Lionel. Oh, look at me, going on like a teenager! Too much bubbly already I'm afraid. But oh well, you'll just have to catch up." Florence firmly gripped Maggie's arms and smiled like she couldn't help it. There's was a natural kinship and there was no resisting it. Maggie felt sure her own smile was just as revealing.

Maggie hugged her friend firmly, thankfully, and nearly felt a tear spring to her eye. God she loved this girl. Sure, she'd had close friends before, but these two had a chemistry, as if they'd always been friends, but had needed to search the world over to reunite. It was effortless and rewarding—a rare combination.

"Come, come," Florence said, and pulled her to the table that sat the man Florence had told her so many intimacies about she could probably write a whole book about him.

The hostess moved away from a private joke she was leant over the table to share with the famed Lionel and that's when Maggie saw him. No. It couldn't be. He looked an awful lot like George.

Mother of God, please don't let it be him. She stumbled for a second on her heel and bent over, as if to straighten it on her foot, but what she was trying to do was blink the image away, so when she stood again there would be Lionel, Florence's boyfriend at the table, and not George, with whom she'd fallen madly in love all those years ago in Fort Bliss, accepted a spur-of-the-moment invitation from to emigrate to Australia, only to then suffer through the worst break-up in history. As far away from home as a person could be.

She'd been "seeing" him a lot lately. There was the bus the other day, and a week before that, a queue at the supermarket checkout. Surely that's all this was.

"Sorry," Maggie said, straightening up. She shook her hair out, which she'd just had cut in a severe bob, before she opened her eyes, trained them at the table ahead and saw George. *Fuck. Fuck, fuck, fuck!* Her ankle gave way.

"Need someone to lean on?" Florence said, took her elbow, and led her directly to George, who apparently was now Lionel, and introduced him as her boyfriend. "Finally, my two favorite people meet!"

George, to his credit, smiled warmly, but gave nothing away. His hair was longer, slightly curly the way it got in the rain. His skin was tanned, as if he'd been surfing every day in his new life. *With Florence. How? How could this be?*

"The infamous Maggie." He stood, went in for her cheek while she braced herself against the swoon that overtook her, the same reaction she always had when he had touched her all those years ago, and then, thankfully, embraced her for a moment while she tried to recover. *George! How could Florence's boyfriend—the one she's been waiting to have pop the question—be George? My George?*

When he disentangled himself, he looked right into her eyes and her throat went dry recalling the dream she'd had earlier that week about just that look, followed by one of his erotic kisses. She tried to blink the image away.

Now was the moment. Own up to it, put it out there. *We used to date.* Laugh over the awkwardness and then move on. They were all adults.

"Where's Reg?" Florence asked before she could think of anything at all to say. George/Lionel scanned the room. Just at that moment Reg came huffing around that same winding route she'd followed the Amazonian hostess along moments prior.

Maggie did her best to smile as she palmed in Reg's direction. When he caught her eye, she could tell he was angry. She shouldn't have left him, and she couldn't exactly explain why she had, but now she had bigger problems.

"I've been calling you, Maggie! You didn't tell me which restaurant it was. There were five right where we got out of the taxi." He was nearly yelling.

"Florence, Riley, this is Reg," she said. Of course she'd told him which restaurant. But what was the point?

Instinctively, she looked into George's eyes, it was as if they'd made some silent agreement: they would not tell. It would be too awkward, or hard, or whatever. Forget that thing about being adults. Instead, she thought, they would take it to their graves. That would be much better.

Visit your favorite bookseller to finish reading Keep Calm and Perfect Your Smolder now!

Milton Keynes UK
Ingram Content Group UK Ltd.
UKHW020835030424
440506UK00008B/845